Madog

BY

GWYN THOMAS

ILLUSTRATIONS BY

Margaret Jones

Contents

page

6   Over the Edge of the World

9   The Court of Owain Gwynedd

17   Three Ships a-sailing

23   Stormy Waters

28   San Zorso, Perhaps

32   The Wonders of the Deep

39   The Isle of Dogs

49   The Dark Ship

56   Inferno

63   The Big Country

70   The People of the New Land

85   Home to Wales

90   Sun Dance

97   The Journey's End

102   Aftermath

1
Over the Edge of the World

Long Barrow was looking after the pigs of his master, Cadwgan the Bighead, on Holyhead Mountain, one day over eight hundred years ago. Looking after the pigs was not very hard work unless they began to wander, or if the weather was wet or cold. On a windy day, the pigs' behaviour could be very strange, and the reason for that – as everyone knew at the time – was that they could see the wind. On this particular day in early May, the warm sun shone down on Holyhead Mountain, and it was so quiet that Long Barrow could hear the flies buzzing about him. The silence and the buzzing made Long Barrow feel very sleepy.

Suddenly, one of the pigs began to grunt and in a while the others joined in and began to squeal. Long Barrow stood up and saw that all the pigs were looking out to sea. 'A sure sign it's going to be windy,' he said to himself. He looked in the same direction as the pigs were staring. There was something there, far out. A breeze began to stir and as it grew stronger, Long Barrow could see that there were ships far out on the water.

He began to gather the pigs together and sent them on before him in a herd that was not easy to control. It was lucky that he knew their tricks and could guess what was going to happen. The best thing was to keep the biggest boar moving down to Holyhead, for Long Barrow knew that the other pigs were bound to follow him, sooner or later.

After reaching level ground, Long Barrow herded the pigs in the shelter of a rock, left them there, and ran to a place where there was a cluster of houses made of wood and turf. As he drew nearer he began to shout, 'Ships! Ships!' As soon as the people round about heard the shouting, the men fetched sickles and pitchforks and made for the seashore – they knew full well what would happen if some wild Irishmen or savage pirates came by.

Eventually, the ships came into view round a rock that stretched down to the water. There were three of them. They slowed a little after coming round the rock and into more sheltered waters. Someone stood up in the prow of the first ship and raised a shield, holding its top end downwards.

'Thank heavens,' said Long Barrow turning to the man next to him.

'A sign of peace,' said the man.

And the men all went down to the water's edge.

'We'll throw ropes,' shouted the man on the prow of the first ship.

'They're Welsh,' said someone.

'They're our ships,' said Barrow, 'the ships of the court at Aberffro.'

Three or four men waded into the water and pulled on the ropes. Some of the sailors, too, jumped down, and helped to pull until the prows of all the ships were dragged far enough up the shore to rest there.

'Thanks for your help, lads,' said the man who had raised the shield and who had by now stepped onto the land. However, he was rather unsteady on his feet.

'He's Cadfan,' said one of the men on shore.

'Correct, friend,' he said.

'But when you sailed, there were seven ships,' the man said.

'Yes,' said he, 'but four of them fell over the edge of the world.'

2
The Court of Owain Gwynedd

By now, Cadfan and his men had reached the court of Owain Gwynedd in Aberffraw ('Aberffro' as it is called in Anglesey). They'd had time to wash and change their clothes, which were so dirty they could stand up on their own. In the court a feast was being held. At one end of the hall there was a platform and the prince and his family and the officers of his court sat at this table, looking down the hall where everyone else sat at tables according to their station. There were fresh, clean reeds on the floor, but the servants waiting on the tables had to keep an eye on two hounds there, just in case they behaved as peasants did, in a way not becoming the dogs of any prince.

At the end of the feast, the bard, Cynddelw the Great Poet, stood up and sang a poem to Owain Gwynedd.

'What's he saying?' Cadfan asked one of the courtiers.

'He's singing the praise of the prince,' he replied. 'He's saying how good he is at bashing people.'

As a sailor, the only words that Cadfan latched onto during the performance were 'anchor' and something about a 'fleet', but he clapped his hands and shouted 'Hooray' with the best of them, after the poet had finished and received a gift from the prince.

After the court steward, a very important officer, had called 'Silence!' and made sure everyone was quiet, the prince, Owain Gwynedd, stood. He was a tall man with a fair complexion and an old scar on his forehead.

'Tonight,' he said, 'instead of a tale, we shall listen to the story of Cadfan and his sailors and how they succeeded in losing four of our ships.'

Cadfan made his way to the front of the hall, his solid body lumbering from one side to the other. His story had better be a good one, because the prince did not sound too pleased with the result of their adventure. Although it was a summer night it was rather dark by now and the light of the fire and the tapers shone brighter as it got darker. Cadfan could see the shining red faces of his audience.

'My lord,' he said, bowing in the direction of Owain Gwynedd, 'thank you for your welcome. It's been a long time since we set off on our voyage on the great ocean. This is how it was. After we left Holyhead, we had a fresh wind behind us and it lasted for three days until Ireland was in sight. We were approaching land when we were confronted by a fleet of ten or more ships. And, when they were near enough to us, some of the sailors on board the leading ships began to shoot arrows. I don't know why, because we've been welcomed in Ireland on more than one occasion. As they had more ships than we did, we decided that the wisest thing to do was to try to make for the open sea again. That was when we caught a strong current flowing towards the south of the island. And going faster than I've ever known, we went past the southern end of Ireland and were pulled out to the sea beyond. A great storm rose, and we were swept out far, far beyond Ireland, until there was no sign of land. We were fortunate that we had enough food and water out there on the ocean, as we tried our very best to take advantage of any winds that could take us back the way we came.

'Four of our ships were carried quite a way from the others. And that was when things really began to go bad. We heard a kind of roaring – quiet at first, but gradually getting louder. And we saw that our ships were being drawn in the direction of the roaring, and that four of our ships were going far more quickly than the other three. The roaring grew louder and louder. And we realized it was the sound of water, like the sound of a waterfall, but that no waterfall was ever this enormous. The next thing we saw was four of our ships moving faster and faster, being pulled towards the roaring. And then... then... the strangest thing that any of us has ever seen happened: four of our ships disappeared over the side of this fall of water. We were all scared as never before, and we began to row like mad. But we sort of remained where we were, because the pull of the current was so great. Some of the crew began to pray and some began to shout and I shouted as well, 'Pull, pull, or we'll all die.'

'We all redoubled our efforts, and as we rowed like madmen the wind rose and pushed us little by little from the waterfall, and it carried us quicker and quicker as we drew further away.

'God and his saints had listened to our unworthy prayers. Our worries were over, and when we came in sight of Ireland, we felt as if we'd arrived back home. As our water and food were very low, we had to land there – the further side from here. There we were welcomed as never before, especially as we told them about the Great Cataract, with

Gavran here,' he pointed to a red-haired man, 'translating for all of us. They also knew about the falls at the edge of the world, and some of them had been near the place, but no one had seen it as we had. We had our fill of food and water, and gathered enough stores for the journey home. We were lucky that we had no trouble with the Irish of the east on our way back. And that is our story.'

You could have heard a flea jump (and there were plenty of those, what with the dogs and some of the courtiers) while Cadfan told his story. But Owain Gwynedd was still staring at Cadfan and making him feel very uneasy. At this moment, Crafanc, the court wizard, stood up to say a few words. Crafanc, which means 'talon', was a good name for him because he was thin and sharp, with long fingers, and his white hair was strong like wires and wild as a storm. But although everyone called him Crafanc to his face, he was known behind his back as 'Ahzedzo'. In a loud, grating voice he said, 'My lord, we as wise men – who have abilities beyond all mortal men – know about these things, the great wonders of creation. I said so [which he pronounced 'Ah-zed-zo'] – of these things before. I said so, as Taliesin, the great hero of all of us wise men, said:

'I have been there.
I have been a book, a document of light,
I have been a lantern in the dark of night,
For a year by my might:
I have been an eagle, an aerie predator,
I have been a bridge over troubled water,
I have been a little boat, a deep sea scouter…'

'Yes, yes,' Owain Gwynedd interrupted him; 'we've heard all that plenty of times. What about the edge of the world?'

'Taliesin had been there. There you have waters, unending waters, falling down, down, down over the edge of the world, into the Other World. And Taliesin has been not only by that falling water, but has also been down, down, down into the Other World. And what a place that is! It is a place of wailing and weeping, of scratching and complaining, amidst serpents and flies and flames...'

Here, the court priest, Beuno, a squat, fat man with a tonsure, interrupted.

'It's not you, but I who am the authority on that place. It is we, as priests, who know about such things. And your Taliesin was never near the place.'

'Yes he was. He's said so. We've learnt his words...'

At this, Madog who was, according to some, the son of Owain Gwynedd – though perhaps he was not – got to his feet. He was a young man of twenty, tall and strong, with yellow hair, a fair complexion and blue eyes; indeed, he looked rather Scandinavian.

'Complete nonsense,' he said. 'If you ask me, there is no waterfall; there is no edge to the world. Indeed, I believe that the world is round. I've sailed beyond Ireland more than once and I've never seen any waterfall, or black hole, or the edge of the world.'

'What!' shouted Crafanc and Beuno and the rest of the court together. 'Round!' Everyone started to laugh and shout, and words like 'Idiot!', 'Nitwit!' and 'Pea-brain!' were clear amidst this shouting.

'Forgive me, my lord,' said Crafanc, 'but I've told you more than once about this boy, that you need to keep an eye on him; I've always said so. I said so when he came to this court – I remember it well – and said that his friend, that Erik from the cold lands of the

north, had given him a piece of iron on a string, a piece of iron that always turned towards the northern star. As if a lump of iron could think; as if a lump of iron could see! I said so – you remember – that it would be a good thing to teach this lad a bit of elementary science. A round world, indeed!'

'Here, my lord,' said Beuno, 'I have to agree with Ahzed… what's said by this man Crafanc. What sense would there be in a round world? How would people, upside down, on the bottom of this round world, not fall off into empty space? And, in any case, even if the world were round, people and ships could fall off the edge just as easily.'

'Not if there is some force in the centre of the world that keeps everyone and everything attached,' said Madog. 'Then nobody would fall anywhere.'

Once again, a great 'What!' went up from Crafanc and Beuno and the rest of the court, and the occasional observation, 'Not all there,' 'Inches short of a yard,' 'A fine lad, I don't dispute, but a bit of a fool.'

'Begging your permission, my lord,' said Beuno, 'I'll offer to instruct this boy in the sciences – mathematics, astronomy, and so on – to keep him on the right path in life.'

'What do you know of that?' snarled Crafanc. 'I said, right from the beginning, that we need to keep an eye on this boy – him and his round world.'

'With a pulling force in its centre! This lad is completely magnetic, if you ask me,' said Beuno.

This was the first time that the word 'magnetic' was used in Welsh, and if we were to look for another word to convey its first meaning it would be 'bonkers' – a word that was coined a little later.

Cadfan raised his voice and said, 'All I'll say is this: if Madog is so sure, why doesn't he go far, far out on the ocean, to see what will happen?' He winked knowingly at some of his fellow-seamen who were in the court.

'Alright,' said Madog, 'give me some ships and I'll go. I'll choose my own men.'

'Well,' said Owain Gwynedd, who was very fond of Madog, 'this could be very dangerous.'

'No more dangerous than fighting the English,' said Madog.

'And expensive,' said Owain.

'We'll help to pay,' said the courtiers – for the first time in living memory.

'If that's so,' said the prince, 'If that's so…' He mused awhile. 'If that's so, I give you my permission to go.'

'That blockhead will see what's what,' said Cadfan under his breath. He was really riled, because what Madog had said had made him out to be a liar. He smiled maliciously at Madog and said, 'Bon voyage!'

3
Three Ships
a-sailing

Erik was a Viking. Two years earlier, he had sailed by himself from Scandinavia and come to land in Anglesey. He was caught by Madog and two of his friends, but they did not kill him. Indeed, he looked like Madog, except that his hair was redder. Madog took to him and they became the best of friends, in spite of Crafanc's scowling and scolding.

'Here's our chance,' said Madog to Erik, the day after the meeting at court. 'We can put to the test what we've been discussing – we can sail off to see the world, go places where no-one has ever been.'

'Will you get permission to build your own ships?'

'I already have,' said Madog, 'and the courtiers have agreed to pay for them.'

'Pay for them! Were they sozzled?' asked Erik.

'They're so sure of themselves,' said Madog. 'They expect us to fall over the edge of the world, or come back in shame.'

'We'll have to put them right, then,' said Erik.

'And to do that, we'll have to build ships,' said Madog, 'and here's our chance to build ships the way you've been talking about them.'

'Where's the best oak? Where are your carpenters?' asked Erik.

'I'll get organized,' said Madog.

In a few days, the prince's foresters had begun to cut down trees. After they had been seasoned for a while, they were sent on ox carts to the court workshops at Aberffraw. Erik, with Madog by his side, supervised the work. It was difficult to find oak trees long enough for the keel, the solid backbone of the ship. Erik hoped that the trees would be long enough for the keels to be made in one piece. They found one that was about the right length, and two others that were a bit shorter. The keel was shaped in a bold curve at the prow, and a gentler curve at the stern. The two ends were planed narrower than the middle of the keel – this made it easier for the ship to cut through the water. The keel was stoutest in the middle as it was there that the ship was at its heaviest. They placed ribs of half-curved timbers every metre or so from the stern to the prow. Planking, not too thick, was nailed to these, overlapping from top to bottom to make the hull watertight. This they smeared on the outside with fat and pitch for extra waterproofing.

The helm, of course, was situated in the stern. To get at the food and drink and equipment in the hold, the decking was removable. On both sides of the ship were the rowlocks. Amidships was a tall mast, secure against the power of the winds. On it was one sail that could be hoisted or lowered according to need. When the sail was hoisted it was held in place with ropes tied to the sides of the ship and to the prow and stern. Over the body of the ship, except for the stern and prow, was an awning that could be raised in rain and bad weather and pulled down in good weather. For extra shelter in bad weather, each sailor had a sleeping bag made of cow hide and wool. Such a long ship could hold nearly twenty tons in weight.

Madog instructed the best carpenter in the court to make a figurehead, a dragon's head, but not too large, in case whoever came their way mistook it for the sign of a warship, and had it placed it on the prow of the main ship. Owain Gwynedd called this main ship *Gwennan Bendragon*. Two other ships were built, not quite as big as the main ship. They were called *Eryn* and *Ffreuer*.

It was a very special day when the main ship was moved from the shipwright's to the sea at the beginning of the following May. There were oxen and horses and strong men, all pulling together, pushing together and grunting together, to get the carts to trundle slowly over a track that had been cleared for the purpose. In a spot where there was deep water near the shore, all made a last concerted effort and the ship slowly slid into the sea, and floated majestically there. After it had been rowed out to water that would not be a lot shallower when the tide ebbed, the ship was anchored in a sheltered cove. Flat stones were carried from Penmon, each stone such that one man could handle it fairly easily, to be used as ballast, to keep the ship from capsizing in turbulent waters. Even Cadfan could not help admiring the vessel, but he made sure that he said to Madog, 'But our ships were nothing like this one.'

'If you want to go far, it pays to have something proper to take you there, in case you find yourself falling over the edge of the world, don't you agree?' said Madog.

'Bon voyage!' said Cadfan once again.

'I'd say his voyage won't be so bonny!' remarked Crafanc. He half-smiled coldly, and others laughed, in surprise more than anything. It was the nearest he'd ever got to cracking a joke.

Once the other two ships were completed, they too were dragged from the workshop to the sea.

In the meantime, Madog and Erik had been busy selecting a crew of experienced sailors and some craftsmen, carpenters and smiths. They needed more than a hundred men to sail the ships. The two combed Anglesey, the shores of Arfon, and Llŷn, to find men of stout heart and good experience. One by one, they succeeded in making up the crews.

Some men refused to contemplate the journey because they knew that the edge of the world was somewhere beyond Ireland.

Madog and Erik would be in charge of the biggest ship *Gwennan Bendragon*. Men called Tudwal and Ynyr would be in charge of *Eryn,* and Elidir and Cynon would be in charge of *Ffreuer.* Tudwal was a giant of a man, with dark hair and a dark beard, and his strength was legendary. Ynyr was smaller but he, too, was dark and sturdy. Elidir was a quiet and thoughtful young man, but was resolute and determined. Cynon was a warrior eager to go on an unusual adventure. He had no equal as a swordsman.

To everyone's surprise, Anwawd, one of the poets of Owain Gwynedd, came to Madog one day and said, 'My lord, it is not proper that a noble person like yourself should go anywhere without a poet to keep a record of your adventures. You could ask me to come with you and if the terms are acceptable, why then, I'd come. I'm an old hand at crossing the Menai Straits in all weathers.'

'You will be paid like a chief poet in the court and, if we discover any treasures, you can have your share of those,' Madog said.

'Paid like a chief poet in the court, and my share of treasures.' Anwawd repeated the terms. 'Hm. Fair enough. I'll fetch my chair.'

'No chairs on board any ship,' said Madog.

'No chairs!'

'There's no room,' Madog explained. 'But you'll have a place to sit.'

'Fair enough, I suppose,' said Anwawd. 'I agree – as long as I'm allowed to bring my harp.'

'Bring your harp, then,' said Madog.

For a month or more Madog and his men sailed the ships around Anglesey and along the Llŷn coastline to see how they performed. They even went through Bardsey Sound in rough weather to put them to a real test.

'In Crafanc's words,' said Erik, 'I said so, didn't I, that all things would be well?'

'Yes,' said Madog, 'and they are.'

After ships and crew had completed the sea trials, the three ships sailed up the Long Strand and dropped anchor not far from Dolbenmaen. Owain Gwynedd was travelling in his kingdom and happened to be in these parts. It was here that the ships were loaded with fresh meats, salted meats, vegetables, water, beer, honey, and wood and iron were taken on board, in case the carpenters and smiths on the voyage would need to repair the ships. They also loaded canvas in case the sails ripped, buckets for baling water, and weapons. Owain Gwynedd and some of his courtiers were there to say goodbye to the crew and to wish them well, but there was no sign of Cadfan. Beuno blessed the voyage and beseeched God to bring them all back safely and to keep them from falling down to hell over the edge of the world. Because Madog sailed from this place, it was called Ynys Fadog, which means Madog's Island.

4
Stormy Waters

It was on a high tide early one fine June morning in the second half of the twelfth century that Madog's sailors rowed three ships down the Great Strand, making for the open sea. Once there, they shipped oars and hoisted the sails to make the most of the wind, which was much stronger on sea than on land. The ships' prows sliced the water, which flowed past smooth and blue. The ships continued on their way through the sea, which was surprisingly calm by day and night. The night sky was cloudless and twinkling with stars, so that the North Star shone clear. By the following morning, the watchman shouted, 'Ireland! Ireland in sight!'

They made for land at Dun Loaghaire. A small gathering of Irishmen and some Scandinavians watched them as they came ashore. Madog greeted this group in Irish, saying that he came from the court of Owain Gwynedd, and that he and his men were going to see how far west they could sail. After welcoming them, a man called Patrick said to Madog, 'Going west! Risking it, aren't you? Haven't you heard about the edge of the world?'

'Yes,' said Madog, 'but we don't think there is such a thing.'

'But everybody says it exists,' said Patrick.

'I'm not so sure myself,' said a large Irishman with a black beard. 'I've sailed far, far to the west, and I never saw anything like any edge, or drop, or anything like that. And, Patrick, remember Saint Brendan,' he said, 'he sailed these seas. It's true he saw wonders, but no edge, no drop, no end of the world.'

Whilst this conversation was in progress, Erik had recognized the Scandinavians from their appearance, and had turned to them.

'Is there anyone here who knows the family of Thorstein, son of Thorbjörn?' he asked in his mother tongue, Norse.

'Who's asking?' said a tall, strong, red-headed man.

'Erik, son of Bjarni the Hunter, from Scandinavia,' said Erik.

'I'm Thorvald, son of Olaf,' said the red-headed man. 'I've heard of your father. Why are you here with Welshmen?'

'I'm here with my friend Madog,' said Erik.

'You've helped him to build these ships.'

'Yes. He saved my life, that's why.'

'That's as good a reason as any,' said Thorvald.

'My father used to say there were many islands towards the south,' said Erik. 'Has any one of you heard about them?'

'I have,' said an old man called Leif.

'Leif sailed far when he was young,' explained Thorvald.

'There are islands, but they're here and there in this great ocean,' said Leif, stretching his arm and pointing to the sea.

'Do you remember any one of these islands?' asked Erik.

'I remember the Isle of Crows, ' he said, 'far off the coast of Gallicia. Then, there was an Isle of Rabbits, to the south. And then, San Zorzo, and Ventura, and Capraria, the Isle of Goats; and the Isles of Canarias. And Inferno, that terrible place. Wherever you go, don't go there. But if you go far enough south, you can make for the west. According to the tales of our people, there are lands to the west; far, far to the west.'

'I was right, then. I was sure I'd heard my father talk of islands to the south,' said Erik. 'And now that you mention it, I recall that name, the Isle of Goats. Thank you.'

The men were welcomed to the court of a lord in Dun Loaghaire. They were given food and drink, and they rested until early the next day. Then Madog and his men went to their ships and sailed from the harbour to the open sea again.

'I hope they're not sailing to their graves in the deep,' said Leif as he watched them sail away.

On open sea Madog set a southerly course, relying on the wonderful magnet Erik had given him and frequently asking his friend for advice. The journey went well for a few days and the wind was fair. Then, one afternoon, the wind turned against them. The ships moved further apart, in case they were hurled against one another; the sails were pulled down, and everything moveable was battened down. The clouds were like black sacks scurrying across the sky, and the sea began to run a terrifying swell. It was a massive task for the helmsmen and their helpers to keep the prows face-on to the waves. One moment the ship would be down in a deep trough, then it would climb the wave moving towards it, higher than a tree. From the crest of the wave the sea round about was clearly visible. Then it was down again; plunging into a pit of emptiness until everyone's stomach was churning, down, down, to face another wave that rose like a white-tipped mountain. Everyone was drenched, and holding for dear life onto whatever solid thing that was at hand. It was one thing to face the waves in daylight, and another thing, and far more terrifying, to face the wrath of the sea in darkness, hoping that the prow was head-on to the waves, and being thrown sideways, at times, until everything was being smashed about you. As this went on and on the fear became overwhelming and the temptation to give up grew stronger, as if death had taken a hold of everyone, and was tightening and tightening its grip. But before daylight the tempest abated and the ships were prancing in the usual way on the uneasy sea. Above, the sky was dark and heavy. This was the first of many storms these sailors had to face.

As the light grew stronger, the seamen realized that the ships were very far from each other and all were in disarray, with everything in a jumble. Some of the food and some of the water on *Eryn* had gone overboard. For two days the crews tried to bring some kind of order to the wreckage and attempted to patch the damage.

'If I had known it was going to be like this, I wouldn't have come,' said Anwawd.

'Shut up and get on with your work like everyone else,' Madog told him angrily. It was no good having anyone complaining, in case the crew began to insist on turning back. And, like several of the other sailors, Anwawd had to get a bucket and start emptying water from the swamped ship.

5

San Zorso, Perhaps

Although Madog had given one of his men the task of cutting a notch on a stout piece of wood each day, to give some idea of the length of their voyage, the wood had been lost in the storm, and so the sailors had only a rough notion of the duration of their passage so far.

Then, one fine day, Erik shouted, 'Land! Land!'

Everyone got to their feet and saw land in the distance. Then they all grabbed their oars and rowed with enthusiasm. As the island – for that is what it was – came nearer and nearer they could see that it was very rocky and that it would be difficult to go ashore there. They had to row for an hour or two before they saw a place where it was possible to disembark. They anchored the ships and most of the sailors swam ashore, after leaving guards to keep watch over the boats until their turn came to put their feet on firm land again. The first thing that Madog did was to order everyone to go down on their knees to thank God for keeping them and bringing them safely to land. '*Bonum est confiteri Domino,*' he said. (That is, 'It is good to praise the Lord.')

One of the first to set foot on shore was Anwawd. He realized that his voyage would provide him with a splendid opportunity to add to his repertoire of tales to recite at court and in great houses after he had returned home – 'If ever that happens,' he said to himself – and he went about, taking careful note of everything he saw.

In the midst of the crying and mewing of many sorts of seagulls, it was his feet, and how they hurt, that first caught his attention. There was no sand on the shore, only pieces of rock and pebbles. As he trod very warily along the shore, he thought how he would describe these when he arrived home.

'We came to an island of rock, far greater in height than Snowdon, with the sea having beaten against it and pulled down great slabs of stones that were as sharp as knives; it was things like that that lay on the shore in the easiest place to land. There were pebbles there as large as our shoes, and what we did was to put these on our feet and tie them with seaweed. After a while, I could slide easily along the shore, saving my feet from being torn.

'We found water there, flowing down out of the rock. It was very clear, and tasted of stones; exceedingly good for quenching thirst. It washed clothes so that they became more colourful. Because it was so hot, we did not have to attempt to start a fire. You only had to leave your clothes on the stones on the shore and, within a couple of minutes, they would be bone dry. The shirt that I washed was so white that I found it difficult to look at it without being blinded. It would be very pleasant to have shades over the eyes to save them from this whiteness that dazzles so.

'After becoming familiar with the shore, several of the bravest amongst us went to climb the rock. It was extremely dangerous, as we frequently had to hang on by our nails over empty spaces, but no harm came to any of us. On top of the rock there was a great forest and flowers of all sorts and colours, and those so bright that we had to shield our eyes with our hands in order to look at them. All around there were bees, every one of them as big as Tudwal's fist, and they made a loud noise, like a cat purring. On some of the trees grew fruits like hedgehogs. You had to be very careful in peeling them as you could easily cut your hands. Their insides are yellow and their taste is sharp and makes your teeth feel dry.

'We cut down two or three trees and sawed them into pieces that could be carried easily and threw them down from the top of the rocks to the sea shore. They would serve well to repair the ships and to provide wood in case of any other damage. In some places there are rabbits, big ones and remarkably tame. They come up to us and rub their noses in our hands. But a few of us could not keep themselves from killing some of them. After lighting a fire by rubbing dry twigs against each other, we had fresh meat for the first time since we left Gwynedd.

It tasted very much like chicken. But even though we had eaten some of them, the poor rabbits did not stop coming up to us.

'After some very pleasant days, Madog was leading several of us up a mountain slope when we heard a deep rumbling from beneath our feet. Then the island started to shake, just as if there was an enormous dragon in the earth waking up and snarling. Before we knew it, the top of the mountain blew up, and fragments of fire fell here and there, as if the dragon were spitting at us. We ran as fast as we could for the rock that went down to the seashore. It was better there; the lumps of fire did not reach that far. We stayed and saw a river of fire beginning to flow down the far side of the mountain and thick smoke rising. It was there that I saw the head of the biggest dragon in the world raising its head over the rim of the mountain and looking down at us with large red eyes. Then, it retreated and began to throw up these rivers of fire that burned as they flowed down to the sea. As soon as the rivers of fire reached the sea, dense black smoke rose up. We only just made it down the rock to the shore and looked for some place to hide, before everywhere became dark, and at mid-day, too. It remained like this for at least two days, before a great wind arose and cleared the black, stinking smoke that choked us and made our eyes burn.

'Madog ordered us to make for the ships immediately. We had been carrying the prickly fruits and rabbits, water and wood to the ships, floating them on pieces of wood lashed together, but there was yet more on the shore, waiting to be carried to the ships. We had to go leaving all of it and everyone was ready to obey Madog's order, and scrambled onto the ships. As soon as we were all aboard, we began to row for the open sea. The last thing we saw was the dragon lifting its head over the rim of the mountain and starting to spit fire and smoke again.'

The Wonders of the Deep

On still days the sailors would fish, and would quite often catch enormous sea creatures which they had to eat raw. Most of the men cut them into small slices and swallowed them. On other still, hot days, most of the crewmen ventured into the sea to swim, keeping close to their own ships. A rope was dragged through the water to make it easier for the men to come aboard if anything unexpected happened.

On one calm day, Madog, Tudwal, Cynon and four others were swimming not far from the ships when they saw a fin cutting through the water. Madog shouted, 'Watch out! To the right.' Tudwal turned in the water and saw a shark drawing near. It was not a very big shark, but was bigger than any shark that you'd wish to meet. As it came near the swimmers, Tudwal dived. He grasped the knife he always carried. He saw the shape of the shark above him, heading for one of the crewmen who was swimming for dear life towards one of the ships, and splashing violently in his fright. Tudwal swam up and struck the shark in its belly with his knife. It began to thrash its tail until the place was awash with foam and blood. Then Cynon arrived, holding onto the rope trailing from one of the ships and he managed to wind it about the tail of the shark. The sailors aboard ship yanked the rope.

By now, Tudwal had raised his head above the water. He sliced the tail of the shark so that a piece of it hung limply from its body by a thin sliver of flesh. The shark was thrashing wildly. While this was going on, Tudwal and Cynon swam with all their might for the nearest ship. The shark made for them, but could not steer itself because its tail had been cut. The men pulled Cynon out so quickly from the sea that it was as if he had jumped out of it. Before Tudwal could be lifted clear the shark got close to him, but two sailors smacked its face with their oars. That enabled the men to get hold of Tudwal and haul him clumsily on board. Then, one of the men pushed the tip of his oar into the mouth of the shark. It closed two rows of savage teeth about it and snapped it like a reed. As there was so much blood in the water, before very long, there were other fins to be seen about the ship, and the sea was alive with sharks, drawn there by the smell of blood. They were biting off chunks of the wounded shark and gulping them down and, before long, there was nothing left of it except shavings of flesh on broken bones in the bloody sea. Then, there was nothing at all there, except the terrifying fins of sharks weaving patterns in the sea. No one went to swim in the sea for a long time after this.

After a few days of easy sailing, the lookout on *Gwennan Bendragon* called he could see cross currents some distance away. Madog ordered the ship to tack, to change direction, but nothing happened; the ships were still sailing forward as if drawn to the white waves of the cross currents. Before long, the ships were turning in circling, boiling seas.

'Try rowing,' said Madog, more in hope than in earnest. They did, but to no avail. The men could do nothing except be whirled around by the boiling sea. They were like this for an hour or so, completely helpless. Then the turbulence ceased. The men could see shoals of fish about the ships, and they trawled them in great numbers. Then the fish disappeared, and an unpleasant silence pressed down on everything. Anwawd was standing near the prow of *Gwennan Bendragon,* and this is how he composed in his head, for use later on, an account of what happened:

'Suddenly there was not a single fish to be seen. They had been there teeming and shining in the sunlight and then there was not a fin left behind. The sea, which had been white and churning, was very, very still, and everyone fell silent. I don't know why. All that could be heard was the timbers groaning softly from time to time. I went to look over the side into the deep. I could see a few bubbles rising. Then I saw something like a green light, as if it were swimming slowly to the surface. This light began to take shape, a large round shape. Then, I realized what this round shape of green light was: it was an eye, an unblinking eye. And this cold, green eye was staring at me. I could feel my body becoming cold all over, and then I could see that this eye was a part of an enormous head. By now, the rest of the crewmen were looking over the side of the ship. A long, dark body stretched out to sea. But what froze everyone's blood was the length of this body in the water. It extended to the far end of our ship, which was the size of a large oak tree. But then, the men on the ship next to us began to point to the water. The body extended to where they were. I looked back over the side, and saw things like long arms stretching out, further than I could see. The great head seemed to swell a little and then became somewhat smaller, as if it were breathing. I could see something like a large beak, like the beak of an eagle, in the head. I don't know for how long I looked down on that cold, green eye. Then, the head swelled more than before, like a pig's bladder full of wind, and the creature disappeared back into the deep. For a while, everyone looked at one another, not able to say anything, and then Madog said a prayer of thanks to God for saving us. After this, he ordered all of us to pull gently on the oars. We moved slowly, without any splashing or flurry, for a long time, and then everyone began to speak at the same time about the monster for which none of us had a name.'

The three ships continued to sail south for days after this. The wind dropped and there was no rain at all. Day after day, the sun was scorching hot, and everyone sought the shade of the awnings. Everything withered under the fierce brightness of the sun, and cracked or blistered and grew pale. The wood of the ships was bleached by the heat, and the bones of all the fish on board became white as snow. Everyone's clothes were bone-dry. They all attempted to protect themselves from the merciless sun. Still, the skin of some of the men was peeled and split. Everyone's lips were hard, and their tongues were rough against the insides of their mouths. Madog had rationed each man to half a cup of fresh water every day and, in spite of all the complaining, that was how it was. The only advantage of the fierce heat was that it killed the usual stench of the ships. No-one wanted much food, and several men grew weak and lost weight. All of them became downhearted and slept for hours by day and night. They were motionless in a desolate sea. This is how Anwawd recorded what happened one day in this unrelenting stillness.

'We were beginning to hope that we would die. We were like withering shadows, and we hardly spoke. We were on the great ocean of death, with nothing to raise our spirits. One day, when most of the crew on our ship were half asleep under the awning, we heard a cry of alarm and wonder from the stern of the ship, and a strange shadow moved across the awning. The helmsman in the stern was looking upwards, with his mouth and eyes wide open. Our eyes and mouths were also wide open, when we looked up. A few metres from our ship, a thick, green neck rose into the air, half as high as our mast. At the end of that neck was a huge serpent's head, with the teeth of a dragon inside a bright red mouth. The serpent opened and shut its mouth rhythmically, as if breathing through it. From its large head two red eyes shone down on us. Sometimes the eyes closed, with half an eyelid moving down from the top of its eyes and half a lid moving upwards from the bottom. The neck was covered in scales and every scale was as big as a man's fist, and its green colour sometimes became a dark blue as the sun shone on it. Behind the serpent was its body, which was twice as long as our ship, with parts of it appearing above the water here and there.

'This sea serpent held its head above water for several minutes. Then, it sank head first and plunged under our ship. We saw its long body dragging behind it, and the whole ship rocked. If that serpent had risen when it was beneath our ship it would have been the end of us, but – thank heaven – that did not happen. It raised its head from the water on the other side of our ship, and swam away, leaving a smooth wake, a wake that spread as it went, slowly at first, and then, more and more quickly, until it disappeared.'

'I knew such creatures existed,' said Erik. 'There are tales of serpents like this in my country. We're lucky it didn't attack us.'

'Thank God that it did not,' said Madog.

Although the men were still scorching in the heat, for a long time after the sea-serpent disappeared they talked about it, and were still afraid for many days, when all was still, they were burning in the sun and almost dying of thirst.

7
The Isle of Dogs

Madog and his men were in the doldrums and endured the searing heat for many days after this, and everyone, except him and Erik thought that this was the end of the journey for them and that they would not come out of here alive. Then, one day they felt a breeze. The men set about hoisting the sails with as much speed as was possible in their weakness. The breeze had freshened by the afternoon and lasted through the night. At mid-day on the following day, the watch in the leading ship, *Ffreuer*, shouted, 'Land! Land ahoy!'

Everyone's heart leapt with joy. The three ships were drawn up beside shores of black sand. All the men jumped out, fell down and kissed that black sand. Once again, Madog offered a prayer, '*Laudate Dominum, quia benignus est.*' ('Praise the Lord, for he is good.') After securing the ships and leaving some men on guard, everyone else made their way up the shore, bearing arms – just in case.

Inland, the black sand gave way to green and fruitful country – at least, some fruit grew on the trees. What they were no-one knew. Clumps of yellow things, like thick fingers, grew on some of the trees. Ynyr pulled on one of these fingers and it came free in his hand. He put it in his mouth and bit it. But he soon spat it out.

'Tastes like old socks,' he said.

He realized that the yellow part was a skin, and that there was something white inside it. He peeled off the skin, threw it away and bit into the white stuff. His eyes lit up, and he began to eat it with relish. When they saw that the stuff was edible, others followed his example, and most of them liked the taste.

'We'll see if there's any water here,' said Madog, 'then we can fill a couple of skins, and send them and some clumps of these fat fingers back to the guards.'

Before long, there was a shout, 'Water!' A clear brook flowed smoothly towards the sea. Everyone made a mad rush towards it.

'Not so fast,' said Madog, 'or you'll be sick.'

Most of the men took his advice and lapped up the water slowly. The two who drank deeply and quickly were soon ill.

'That's how it is when you don't listen,' said Erik. And although the wretches were very poorly, they got no sympathy.

'You two can take water and fruit back to the guards,' said Madog.

'And be as sick as you will on the black shore!' said Erik.

After a week the sailors had recovered and began to explore the island. One day Madog and Cynon were leading the way, with a dozen men following them, when they saw a number of huge dogs in the distance. Madog shouted, 'There are dogs... or wolves over there.' As he said this he drew his sword. Elidir came to him. 'They're dogs,' he said, 'but bigger than any dogs I've ever seen.'

The dogs sat looking at them, without moving.

'Can we venture a bit further?' Elidir asked.

'Why not?' said Tudwal, who had caught up with Madog and Cynon. And on they went. The dogs had not moved, but now they began to bark. Then, suddenly, all of them – six in all – got up together and started to run towards the sailors, barking savagely. By now, the men in front, all except Tudwal, had their swords ready. The first dog made a leap for Madog. Its teeth were white and long and there was white foam about its mouth. With his sword Madog struck its head, until it split open, gushing blood. Tudwal had grabbed another dog by the throat. He whirled it about three or four times and then let go, so that it sailed through the air and crashed head first against a rock. Elidir was having some difficulty with another of the dogs; it had fastened its teeth in his cloak, and was tugging fiercely at it and snarling viciously. Cynon came to Elidir and plunged his sword in the dog's side. It squealed loudly, let go of the garment and turned on Cynon, but to no avail; its head was also split open. Tudwal killed another dog with his knife, and Elidir wounded the fifth of them so that it looked wretched. There was one dog left, a large, black brute that dropped to the ground to gather its strength to leap. It snarled and kept its eyes fixed on Cynon.

'Leave this one to me,' said Tudwal, as he stood between Cynon and the dog.

Its frenzied eyes were upon him by now and, with a deep snarl, it made a leap for Tudwal's throat. With his large fist he gave the dog a blow on the side of its head, and it whined as it flew through the air to the ground. It came down heavily and awkwardly, but it turned with astonishing speed and made for Tudwal again. When it was in mid-leap, an arrow hit it in the guts. One of the men following had seen what was happening. The dog fell in a heap by Tudwal's feet, twitched helplessly, and died.

'Thank you very much!' said Tudwal sarcastically. 'I was shaking in my boots!'

'You did the right thing,' said Elidir to the bowman, as he caught up with them. Then he smiled and added, 'You saved Tudwal a great deal of trouble!'

'We know there are dogs on this island,' said Cynon. 'I wonder whether there are any people here.'

'The best thing to do is to go back to the others, in case they're caught out without our knowing about it,' said Madog.

By the time Madog and his companions returned to the shore, where, by now, a camp had been set up within sight of the ships, nothing out of the ordinary had happened, but two men who had been exploring along the shore said there were signs of coming and going in the woods, about two miles from the camp.

'We'll go and have a look there tomorrow,' said Madog. 'I want all of you to eat your fill of these yellow apples we've gathered. They seem to be good for the skin, and they help to heal wounds.'

'They're far tastier once you peel off the skin. Then the fruit breaks into pieces in the shape of a new moon,' said one of the sailors.

'You heard that, didn't you?' said Madog. 'We'll all do the same.'

The next morning a small number of men were left in the camp to keep an eye on things while the rest went to look around, with the two who had seen signs of activity leading the way. As they came nearer to the spot, Madog had the feeling that someone was watching him. Then, quietly and suddenly, as if the trees and bushes before them had woken up, there stood a row of men, looking at them. Their skin was dark but their hair was fair. They were wearing clothes made of leather and plaited reeds, and in their hands they held primitive knives and spears. The two groups of men stood eyeing each other for several minutes. Then, one of the natives approached, step by step, and very warily. He placed his hand on his breast and said, 'Gwanshe'.

Madog stepped forward, equally warily, placed his hand on his breast and said, 'Madog'.

Then the native pointed to his men and said again, 'Gwanshe'.

This time, Madog pointed to himself and said very clearly, 'Madog'. Then, he pointed to his men and said, 'Welsh'.

The native then pointed to his men and said, 'Gwanshe,' and then pointed to himself and said, 'Cano'.

Madog pointed to the sea and made an up and down motion with his hand, to suggest a voyage over the waves, and pointed towards the far distance. Cano put down his weapons and came nearer. Madog also put down his sword and stepped towards Cano. The native indicated that Madog should follow him. His men separated and made way for his sailors to follow Madog. They did so, cautiously, but all the time they kept nodding pleasantly to the natives.

After walking a mile, they came to a glade, where there were houses made of wood and reeds, set in a circle. In the middle, there was a great fire with meat roasting on it. The Welsh recognized the smell of roast pig. By making signs with his hands, Cano suggested that the Welsh should sit down on one side of the fire, and his men did likewise on the other side. Then girls came out of the houses, wearing clothes made of plaited reeds, and began to carry fruits in dishes for everyone who was there, starting with the Welsh, and smiling agreeably on all. Next, they began to slice the meat into portions, putting them on earthenware plates and distributing them, as with the fruits. Everyone began to eat merrily. Then, they brought them drink in earthenware cups.

'Don't overdo it with the drink, lads,' said Madog, all the time smiling pleasantly on Cano, and drinking from his cup. Cano raised his own cup to his mouth and finished it off in one draught. That is what all his men did, as well. The girls brought them more drink, and they did the same with that, and, in spite of Madog's warning, some of the Welsh began to do likewise. And so it went on. After a while, the natives stood up and formed a circle, encouraging the Welsh to do the same. The natives began to dance and chant and indicated that the Welsh should join in. All the while, the girls came and went with the drink. As they drank and sweated, several of the Welsh began to feel peculiar. Anwawd went to stand on a boulder and began to recite poetry, not very well, as it happened. As they saw this, all the natives stopped, and listened carefully, and then bowed down before him and prostrated themselves on the ground, and the dogs began to howl. Cano held Madog's arm and, pointing towards Anwawd, said, 'Banee. Banee.'

'Shabby, shabby,' said Madog, shaking his head apologetically.

'Banee mohooboo,' said Cano, 'Banee mohooboo.'

'Banee mohooboo?' asked Madog, perplexed.

'Banee mohooboo,' said Cano emphatically.

'This performance by Anwawd must mean something to them,' said Elidir to Madog.

'I thought that, too,' said Madog, 'but mean what?'

'This may have something to do with it,' said Ynyr.

Six strong men came in, carrying a large woman on a kind of bed. She was dressed rather skimpily in sheaves of reeds that showed more of her ample body than they concealed. The woman smiled, displaying two teeth, one a shade of white and one black.

'Banee mohooboo,' said Cano pointing to her.

'Oh!' said Madog. As he saw her being transported in Anwawd's direction, Madog turned to Elidir and said, 'Is she going to eat him, or marry him: that is the question.'

In the meantime, Anwawd recited like a man inspired; he had never had such a reception before. But he had not noticed the arrival of the great lady. When she was brought before him, he stopped in mid-sentence.

'Banee mohooboo,' said the woman, smiling broadly, as she was put down gently. Then she began to dance, wiggling her bountiful attractions. Anwawd stared at her in open-mouthed wonder for a while, and then motioned that she should go away, so that he might proceed with his recitation.

'Dragon of Anglesey,' he said, 'how brave was…'

'Anakoo noggin,' said the woman.

'I suspect that the natives expect Anwawd to take her off their hands,' said Elidir.

'Yes,' said Madog. 'He must have done something, or said something to make them think that.'

At that, the great lady struggled to the top of the boulder with Anwawd. As Anwawd had drunk more than he should have, he was not alert enough to realize what was happening. The great lady tried to hold him in a bear-hug. Anwawd pushed out his belly and bumped her so that she fell heavily on her behind. Everyone fell silent.

'Banee nawanee mohooboo,' said Cano in amazement, and all the natives began to

laugh. The Welsh laughed too, to be courteous. This was the very worst thing they could have done, for it was one of the natives' beliefs that no-one ought to laugh except on special occasions. Still laughing, Cano attempted to strike Madog. But he was sober enough to avoid the blow.

'Get going, get going now, lads!' ordered Madog, and the lads made an attempt – a spectacularly messy one – to run away. They were lucky that the natives were scarcely any more sober than they were, and their attempts to give chase were even more messy.

The men in the camp were lying around when they saw Madog and his companions running towards them, as they thought, in extreme disarray. Then they saw strange men running hither and thither in an attempt at pursuit. The guards were extremely fortunate that they had carried fruits and water on board ship during the day, so when their fellow-mariners arrived, every effort was made to get them aboard before the natives arrived. Only a few of them had remembered to bring arms with them, and their aim, as they cast what spears they had, was woefully awry. When the ships had gone far enough from the shore for everyone to feel safe, they looked back at the black sand. The great lady was clearly to be seen there and, on the wind came a lucid cry, 'Banee mohooboo! Banee mohooboo!'

8
The Dark Ship

For many days after this, Madog and his men were blessed with favourable currents and swift winds that took them westward, the direction Leif had suggested in Dun Loaghaire. Madog's lodestone pointed north, so he could work out where the west was. Eventually, they came to blue, clear waters full of a type of seaweed, where the currents were sluggish. They had to row every day in this sea. During the day things were not all that bad, but at night the men became uneasy. Everyone who kept the night watch or had been awake at night insisted that they felt that there were some very unpleasant things in the waters. Madog himself kept watch one still moonlit night. He was in the prow of the ship and could see the other two ships clearly. He began to feel that there was something in the water. He looked over the side of the ship. After a while, he caught a glimpse of phosphorescence in the deep, and soon after caught another glimpse. He stared and saw, for an instant, shapes interweaving. 'Snakes!' he said to himself. 'Fiery snakes.' He looked again, but caught only an occasional glimpse of them. He began to think, 'What if these crawled aboard ship?' A cold shiver ran down his back. He examined the boards of the deck as best as he could by the light of the moon but there was nothing moving there, thank goodness.

The following morning, Madog ordered his men to row near enough to *Eryn* and then to *Ffreuer* to ask the night-watch on both ships whether they had seen anything out of the ordinary during the night.

'Sometimes there's a cold light in the water,' said one.

'I didn't see anything,' said the other, 'but something certainly makes me feel uneasy.'

Madog told the men what he had seen in the water.

'Can snakes swim?' asked one of the sailors.

'Some of our people,' said Erik, 'talk of poisonous snakes in some seas.'

'We'll have to be careful,' said Madog, 'and have three men on watch in every ship at night.'

That night, Madog decided to keep watch again with two of his crew. Ynyr and Cynon, with others, kept watch on their ships. Once again, it was a pleasant, still, moonlit night, until the flashes of phosphorescence began to appear, and dark shapes moved in the water. Sometimes, they would be close up to the ships, but there was no sign that they made any attempt to slither on board. This is how it was for the greater part of the night, and then, as the night came to an end, Ynyr bent over the side of his ship and thrust a spear into the sea. He raised it gingerly from the water, without trying to bring it on board. Something was writhing on the point of the spear. After it was light, the men on the *Eryn* made a circle on the deck with ropes and pieces of wood. Ynyr lifted a snake of about two metres in length over the side of the ship and put it in the circle. Its back was black and its belly bright yellow. Everyone was ready for any movement, but after the snake had been put on the deck, although it was still alive, it could not move with any ease.

'It's a sea-snake,' said Tudwal, 'it doesn't move well on anything dry.'

'That's some comfort,' said Ynyr. 'If it can't move with any ease here, then there's little chance that it can climb up the side of the ship.'

'Can we eat it, do you think?' asked one of the men.

'Have a go if you like,' said Tudwal, 'but don't expect me to touch a bit of it.'

'It may be that you're right,' said the sailor; 'whatever it tastes like, it is disgusting to look at.'

Ynyr killed the snake, after everyone on the other ships had seen it, and he threw it back into the sea.

You would expect the nights to be a bit better now that everyone knew that there was little danger of the snakes climbing on board ship but, strangely enough, this knowledge did not make the nights any less uneasy. Elidir was on watch one night when the moon was on the wane and almost half full. There was a heavy silence all around him. The occasional glimpses of flashes in the water were of no help to put him at ease, but at least he now knew what was there. This unease was different. It was a feeling that there was someone on the sea behind him, watching him, but when he turned to look, there was nothing there. Then, he heard a low sound, as if someone were in pain and groaning. This lasted for a second or two. He turned again: nothing. As he turned to look back, between

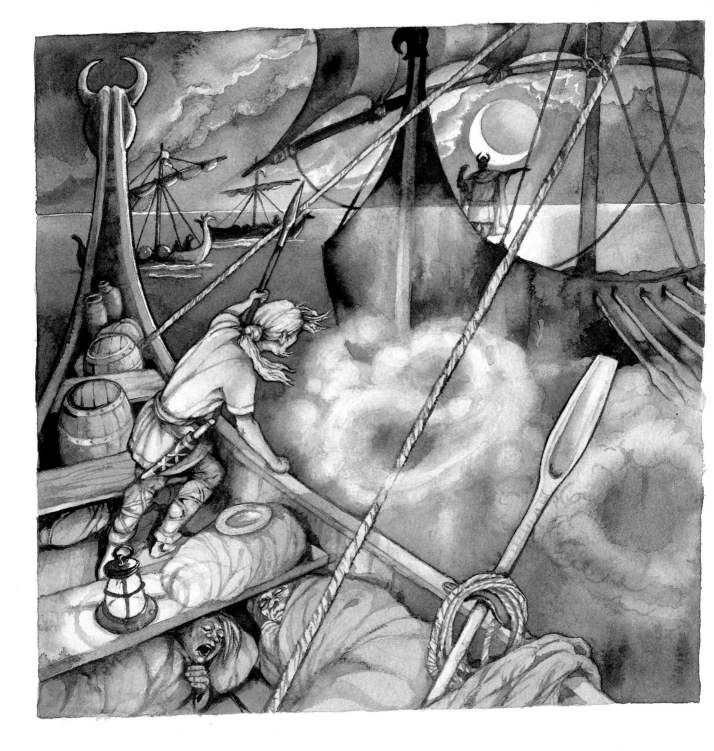

him and the moon he saw the dark shape of a ship. It was a bigger vessel than any of theirs. The sound came again for a few seconds. On board the dark ship, in the prow, was a shape like a man. Then, there was nothing there. When the bright morning came, he began to suspect that he had not seen anything at all.

The next man to see the dark ship was Madog himself. The moon was still waning and there was a silvery, cold light on the sea when he, too, heard the moaning. Between him and the moon, he saw a ship and, indistinctly, a shape like the shape of a man on the prow. He saw the shape for long enough to make out that he raised his arm and beckoned him to follow. Then everything disappeared.

The next morning, Madog ordered the ships to row near enough to each other for him to address the sailors and for them all to hear him.

'Men,' he said, 'there's something strange in these waters.'

The sailors began to feel uneasy; to be on the sea and far from any land was enough of a strain.

'Not more snakes?' asked one sailor.

'No,' said Madog. 'Has anyone of you heard or seen something at night?'

There was silence for a while, then Elidir said, 'I have.'

'What?'

'A groaning sound. A dark ship.'

One could see fear and terror gripping the strong, tough men, and some of them made the sign of the cross.

'Anything else?' asked Madog.

'I can't be certain,' said Elidir.

'Was the ship empty?'

'No, no, I don't think so.'

'What did you see?'

'Something that looked like a man.'

There was another wave of fear among the men, and more signs of the cross.

'Nothing else?'

'Nothing.'

'There's something very strange here,' said Madog.

'The ship is a spectre,' said Erik. 'There are stories about things like this, illusions and noises that drive men mad.'

The men were again disturbed.

'What can we do?' they said.

'Pray to God,' said Madog. 'Now, listen carefully. Whatever there is on that ship is beckoning. He wants us to follow him.'

'We must not do that on any account,' said Erik.

'I agree,' said Madog. 'If anyone sees this thing beckoning, he must tell the rest of us in which direction he is beckoning. We must go in another direction entirely. He beckoned to me, last night, to follow him in that direction. We won't go that way. Erik, use the iron to take us in the opposite direction.'

That is what happened. On the last night, when anyone saw the black figure on the dark ship, he was still beckoning in the same direction. The day after he was last seen, the sailors felt a pulling power in the waters, and they had to double the strength of their rowing not to be drawn with the current. The water could be seen whirling round, and they could hear a roaring flood far off.

'It's a whirlpool,' said Erik, 'the biggest whirlpool that anyone has ever seen. Pull, lads, pull.' It took an extraordinary effort, but gradually the effect of the water subsided.

Three days later, they saw land again.

'Thank God,' said Madog, and he offered up a prayer.

9

Inferno

After they came ashore, everything went well, at first. There was plenty of fruit on this island, and plenty of water, in pools, and the carpenters were able to repair the ships and fashion new oars from the wood on the island. The sailors began to explore the land. One day, Madog led one crew in one direction and Erik led another crew in a different direction. A half a dozen men were left on the shore near the ships to keep guard. Anwawd was one of them.

After spending some time seeing to the ships' gear and tackle and making sure that the work on the sails had been done, the sailors began to play a game they had devised, which consisted of throwing a small stone on the beach and then seeing who could throw larger stones next to it. After tiring of this, one by one, they began to wander along the shore, keeping sight of the ships. They found a stretch of land covered with green growth.

'I wonder whether this green stuff is edible,' said one sailor.

'Be careful,' advised Anwawd, 'in case it's poisonous.'

'I'll try a tiny piece,' said the sailor.

'A very, very small piece,' said Anwawd.

The sailor broke off a leaf and put a tiny piece in his mouth.

'It's sweet,' he said, 'very sweet.'

'Don't taste any more of it,' said Anwawd. 'We'll wait and see what happens.'

What happened next was that the sailor lay down. After a while, a wide smile appeared on his face.

'How do you feel?' said Anwawd.

'Like,' said he, 'like…'

'Like what?'

'Like an angel.'

'Angel? What do you mean, like an angel?' asked Anwawd.

'High in the sky, above the world,' said the sailor dreamily, 'in a land of many colours. I am… I am…'

'You're what?'

'At ease…'

'He doesn't make sense,' said Anwawd.

By now, the other sailors had tried the leaves and they, too, were beginning to talk nonsense.

'Come here, luvvy,' said one.

'Who?' asked Anwawd.

'This girl who's coming towards me,' he replied.

'A girl coming towards you! And where is she?' asked Anwawd, losing patience.

'Here, of course,' he answered. 'Can't you see her, wearing the sun, all gold and tender?'

Anwawd was surprised for he had never heard this man say anything but short sentences, and those as lacking in imagination as a brush. He felt as if the man were tramping into his territory, and beginning to wax poetical.

'Let me see,' said Anwawd, and chewed a large piece of leaf.

When, at the end of the afternoon, the two crews came back from their reconnaissance, they came upon the guards, stretched out, awake, all of them with silly smiles, and some of them attempting to sing, without much success.

'What's wrong with these fools?' asked Madog.

'They look as if they're plastered,' said Erik.

'Plastered on what?' asked Madog.

'On the white lily of the valleys, the radiant roses of the vales. Come with me, my darling love,' said Anwawd, with feeling.

'Who's he talking to?' asked Tudwal.

'With someone in his dream,' said Elidir.

'But his eyes are open,' said Tudwal.

'That may be, but he's not with us,' said Elidir. 'The whole lot of them must have drunk something, or eaten something.'

'I'll take the largest portion of that pig,' said another of the dreamers. 'And fill this cup with the red wine.' Then he added, 'Not that wine, you ass; the other.'

'This is serious,' said Madog. 'What if someone had attacked our ships, with this lot here dreaming!'

'Precisely,' said Erik. 'But we'll have to wait for them to recover before doing anything.'

'Carry them back to camp,' ordered Madog.

It was the next day when the dreamers awoke. All they could remember was that they had eaten some leaves, that the taste was sweet, and that they had been somewhere that was very pleasant.

'No more of this,' said Madog. 'We'll stay here today, to keep an eye on this lot.'

By mid-day, those who had been dreaming began to become agitated, and to beg for just a little bit more of the leaves.

'No,' said Madog.

Then they began to behave as if they were terrified of something.

'Let me be, let me be,' they cried.

'I'll try and have a word with Anwawd,' said Madog. 'He's the most sensible of them, or is supposed to be, at least.'

'What's wrong?' he asked.

'Someone's coming,' said Anwawd, his eyes full of fear.

'Who's coming?' asked Madog.

'From the dark caves,' said Anwawd, 'I can see her.'

'Who's she?' asked Madog.

'That girl I saw yesterday.'

'But you liked her.'

'She's changing,' said Anwawd. 'She's changing into... into a serpent. Her two legs are coiling into one, and she's fallen down. She's writhing there and turning green, and she's covered with scales. Her head's turning pointed, and twisted out of shape. Her eyes are turning red. She's seen me... and is slithering towards me, heaving her fat length forward over the ground. Some yellow stuff is dripping from her teeth... It's poison. She's coming, coming.'

Anwawd began to make a desperate attempt to run away. It took three men to hold him down. He was the worst of the lot, but by now other dreamers were also causing difficulties.

'I've got an idea,' said Elidir. 'It may be that if we went where they were yesterday and fetched some of those leaves and gave some to them they'd quieten down.'

'What then?' asked Madog.

'What then is not important,' said Erik, 'but what now. We have to do something.'

'Then go and fetch some,' said Madog to Elidir. 'But only a little.'

It did not take long for Elidir to gather a few leaves. A very small amount was given to every one of the dreamers and, within a few minutes they had become quiet and were smiling as stupidly as they had the previous day.

'These leaves are extremely dangerous,' said Madog. 'They conjure beautiful dreams, and then the most terrible nightmares. Now, no one else, no one, is to taste any of these leaves. We've got enough trouble on our hands with these six. We have to try and bring them round without giving them any more of these leaves.'

The six dreamers were seven times worse than they had been during the morning. Sometimes they shouted wildly, at other times they wept in fear, and, once more, they threatened all around them.

'A big man, a huge man is coming,' shouted Anwawd. 'He's beginning to change. Horns are growing out of his head. His head's getting larger and larger and turning into a bull's. He's scraping the ground with his back legs and starting to move towards me. He's coming, coming.' Anwawd screeched and then moved like a man being gored by a bull. Next, it seemed he had fainted, or as if he was about to die. Then he became agitated again and shouted, 'The giant birds are coming.'

'We'll have to give them more leaves,' said Elidir.

'No,' said Madog. 'They're getting worse. We'll have to let them be, and see what happens.'

'Claws! Claws!' Anwawd shouted, looking to the sky and pointing at something. 'An eagle in the sky and a lion, an eagle that is also a lion. He's coming.'

He behaved as if a savage creature were attacking him, and he screeched until he was hoarse. Then he wept as if it were the end of the world.

'The woods, the woods,' shouted another of the dreamers. 'There are bats as big as cats growing on the trees. Their mouths are covered in blood, in blood. They're falling from the trees like ripe fruit and starting to fly. They're coming, coming. Look out. Here they are.' He attempted to keep something from him, and then grasped his throat and screamed.

'They're being killed many times over in their nightmares,' said Elidir.

'Yes; as if they were in hell,' said Madog, 'being killed over and over, and not dying.'

'This is the Inferno that Leif talked about,' said Erik.

'Are they lost forever: that's the question,' said Elidir.

'That's what I was wondering,' said Madog. 'We'll have to tie them down and see what happens.'

And that is what they did.

The night was a turbulent one. Every so often, the dreamers would shout and groan, and then scream, while making a great effort to free themselves and escape. But no-one can escape his nightmares without awaking, and these men could not wake up.

In the morning, they were covered in sweat, and there were red marks on their arms and legs, where the ropes had been, but they were quieter and, in the heat of the sun, all of them fell asleep. When they woke up, one by one, they could not understand why they had been tied up. They did not remember what had happened to them.

'Just as well,' said Madog. 'If they did remember, they could go mad.' Then he added, 'We'd better leave this place. It's more dangerous here than any of us imagined.'

10
The
Big Country

It did not take long for them to come out of the 'seaweed ocean', as the sailors had begun to call it, and they were fortunate to have a fair east wind. One morning, a seagull perched on top of the mast of *Eryn*, one that they had not seen its like before. A flock of them gathered about the three ships the following day.

'All of these are signs,' said Madog, 'that there's land out there to the west.'

That night, the lookout on *Gwennan Bendragon* shouted, 'Light.' Although his shout disturbed the sleep of the sailors, they were glad to be woken.

'Is that the light of a fire?' asked Madog.

'Looks like it,' said Erik.

'Who lit that, I wonder?'

'God willing, we'll know before long,' said Erik.

The next morning, all the men were excited; they could smell something fresh instead of the sea smells, of which they were sick and tired. Presently, some greenery appeared in the distance, as if rising from the sea far away.

'Land! Land ahoy!' shouted the men on watch on all three ships.

'Hurrah! Hurrah!' shouted everybody.

As they came nearer, they pulled down the sails and rowed the last hundred metres or so, and then the bottom of the first ship, *Gwennan Bendragon,* scraped lightly on a sandy shore. Madog jumped into the sea and walked the few metres to the land. When he arrived, he went down on his knees, kissed the sand, and offered a prayer of gratitude to God, '*Gloria Patri, et Filio, et Spiritu Sancto*' ('Glory to the Father, and the Son, and the Holy Ghost.'). It did not take long for the sailors of the three ships to follow him. They had come to land again; they had not fallen over the edge of the world!

As always, the first task after coming to land was to secure the ships and to leave men to guard them. Then two parties of men went to explore the land. They walked with the unsteady gait of seamen who had spent months at sea. They found streams of fresh water. After filling the skin bags with water, they hid them and ventured slowly into a forest. They saw a stag, but it disappeared before anyone could string an arrow. They were more lucky with rabbits; because they were so easy to catch – they caught about forty. They also gathered berries and nuts, before going back to fetch their water-skins and returning to the seashore.

By the time they arrived the guards had lit a fire, made by rubbing two sticks together and then setting alight dry grass and wood. That night, they all enjoyed a feast that they remembered for a long time, and everyone found the taste of the meat and fruit particularly pleasant. The awnings from the ships were fetched ashore in order to make tents, but most of the men preferred to sleep under the stars rather than in the smell of canvas that was still full of sea salt.

The first morning on this mainland was fine and warm. The guards had not seen anything untoward during the night. All of the men wanted to wash in fresh water. Some of the two crews who had gone searching the previous day were bent on building a dam on one of the streams, to form a pool, but others wanted to follow one of the streams and search for pools. The final decision was that they would search for pools. After walking for half a kilometer, they came upon a deep, clear pool, with plenty of space in it. Everyone jumped fully clothed into the water and, after splashing there and playing about, they came out and hung their clothes on bushes to dry before going back into the water.

After being there for a good hour they came out, and went to look for their clothes.

'Where's my shirt?' shouted one sailor.

'And my trousers?' said another.

'Some joker's stolen my shoes,' shouted another.

Most of the men dressed quickly. Since all the sailors had been in the water, it was not possible that some of them had been playing tricks, and so everyone was especially careful; there were strangers about.

'We'd better go back to camp,' said Madog. 'We don't know what could be hiding in these trees.'

'Someone who's wearing my shirt,' said one seaman.

'And my trousers,' said another.

The men withdrew cautiously, looking behind them all the time, but they saw no one.

After reaching the camp and recounting what had happened, the guards said that they had seen nothing.

'We'll double the guard tonight, ' said Madog, 'and we'll load food and water onto the ships, in case we have to flee.'

And that is what they did.

During the night, the guards saw lights some distance inland, the lights of fires, like the one they had seen from the sea. The guards awoke everyone, but nothing happened.

'We'll stay around the camp today,' said Madog.

'I'm quite willing to take a few men and see what we can find,' said Tudwal.

'I'll go, too,' said Cynon.

'No, we'd better not,' said Madog.

The sailors spent the day swimming, playing at throwing spears, and practising with their swords on the shore, but they placed guards to keep an eye on the land and the sea. At about mid-day, the guards from the landward side came to the middle of the camp. They did so without any commotion, and without hurry.

'There are men on the hill,' said one guard quietly to Madog.

'Go and tell everybody,' he said, 'and tell them not to get jumpy, but to pretend that they're carrying on with whatever they're doing.'

Madog looked towards the hill. He could see about twenty men there, and he could see that they were colourfully dressed. By now, all the sailors knew that they were being watched by strangers, strangers who did not attempt to hide. In spite of Madog's orders, the men's activities slowed down, and everybody stood and looked up to the hill.

'I'm going over there,' said Madog.

'I'll come with you,' said Erik.

'No,' said Madog. 'I'll go on my own. If anything happens to me, you will be responsible for the men. Be ready to make a run for the ships.'

'We'll stand and fight,' said Tudwal.

'Better not,' said Madog.

He began to walk across the shore, towards the hill. He walked slowly and it was obvious that he had no weapons.

As he came nearer to the green land that came down to the shore, one of the men on the hill began to walk down to meet him. Madog saw a tall, powerful young man. His skin was dark with a tinge of red in it. Across his forehead there was a red line, and on each of his cheeks a black line. He had thick dark hair, which had been plaited with a reed or moss, and in it there were three striking feathers. He wore something like an apron made of deerskin, as far as Madog could see, and on his belt there were bright metal discs. He had no shirt. He had no weapons either, for he stretched out his arms as he drew near to Madog, to show this. Madog raised his arms, too, to show he had no weapons either.

After he had reached Madog, the young man raised his right hand with its palm towards him and said, 'How!'

Madog did likewise and said 'How!' Then, Madog pointed to the sea and said the word, 'Voyage.'

'Voyage,' said the young man. His accent was perfect. Then he pointed to the land behind him and said, 'Tchikee,' (which meant 'home').

'Tchikee,' said Madog. His accent too was perfect. Then he pointed to himself and said, 'Madog,'

The young man then pointed to him and said, 'Madog,' and then he pointed to himself and said 'Isticáti,' (which meant 'of the colour of the sun').

Madog then pointed to him and said, 'Isticáti.' Then Madog held out both his hands, raised them in the direction of the hill, and brought them together. Then he pointed to his camp and said, 'Welsh.'

Isticáti understood immediately and shouted a few words. Twenty men came down, all of them carrying weapons that looked like knives. Isticáti pointed to them and said, 'Calusa'. Then Madog and Isticáti began to walk together down to the camp. As they approached, Madog shouted, 'Put down your weapons.' The sailors did so, albeit with some reluctance. Although Isticáti's face did not convey much, Madog thought he was pleased.

After they had arrived in the camp, Madog said to his men, 'Do as I do,' and held out his arms. When they saw the sailors do this, Isticáti's men put down their own weapons, and made the same sign. Madog took them to the ships. They showed great interest. Then Isticáti called one of his men. He came and pulled out something like a cow's horn from his belt and blew into it, making a loud noise. Isticáti pointed to the sea, and soon they saw two boats made of tree trunks, with three men in each boat, coming towards them from behind a headland. They beached the boats, and Madog and Isticáti's men examined and admired each others crafts, making themselves partially understood with signs.

'Start roasting rabbits,' said Madog to two of his sailors. 'And you,' he said to two others, 'bring berries and fruits here.'

When he saw these preparations, Isticáti said something to his men, and two of them went to the boats and brought a haul of big fish from them. They gave these to the two cooks. Every member of the Calusa took a great interest in the cooking, often made remarks to each other, and showed surprise and wonder from time to time.

Before everyone sat down in a large circle, Isticáti said something to one of his men, and he ran swiftly to the edge of the shore and up the hill. He returned with another man following him. He was wearing on his head the trousers that had been stolen the previous day. He had shoes on his feet, but had pushed his legs into the arms of the shirt and was wearing it as trousers. When they saw him, everyone started to laugh.

When the food was ready, all of them enjoyed a friendly feast on the shore of this foreign land.

11

The People of the New Land

Isticáti and his men stayed the night in the camp. Then, by signs, Isticáti made it known that he wanted Madog and his men to come with him. Madog indicated that he was worried about his ships. What happened then was that Isticáti's men fetched tree trunks, and after unloading the ballast and keeping it in a particular spot, with the help of the Welsh, they rolled the ships up the shore on these logs. Then, the Calusa began to disguise the ships with greenery until there was no sign of them.

After finishing this task, which took a long time, Madog and his crew went with Isticáti and his men. They walked for an hour or more. They came at last to a clearing in the thick woodland at the foot of a high hill whose top was flat and treeless. It was a fire on top of this hill that the sailors had seen from their ships. The natives used the fire to make their clothes sweeter, and to drive out red beetles from them. In the glade stood several buildings of wood and skins, raised above ground level, and with wooden floors. As Madog and his men arrived, everyone came out and stared at them in wonder. That night, a great feast was held.

When all the men were seated for the feast, Isticáti raised his hands in the air and spoke some words of prayer, as it was obvious to the Welsh. Then, from one of the cabins, a man clad in many colours emerged. He had an apron made of deer skin, a head-dress of many feathers, and his body was painted with long lines of amber and red, and he had one white line down his nose. He walked into the circle of men, slowly and with great dignity, before standing in the middle.

'Ah-zed-zo' (which meant, in the Calusa language, 'most wise') said Isticáti, pointing to him.

'Ah-zed-zo?' asked Madog.

Isticáti nodded and repeated, 'Ah-zed-zo.'

Madog could see that many of his men had their hands by their mouths to hide their smiles, because they remembered the 'Ah-zed-zo' in the court of Owain Gwynedd.

'What did he say?' enquired Anwawd, who was sitting next to Madog, and had brought his small harp with him.

'Ah-zed-zo,' said Madog.

'Ah-zed-zo! Well blow me down! Who would have thought that our old friend had got here before us!' said Anwawd. Then he added, 'This one looks as stupid as our own Ah-zed-zo.'

'Shsh!' said Madog, beckoning him to be silent.

But Ah-zed-zo had heard, and had gathered that things were being said about him. He came over to Anwawd, gathered a handful of dust from a small bag on his belt, and blew it into the poet's face.

'Now see here, Ah-zed-zo,' said Anwawd, half getting up, until he was prevented by Madog.

'Nowsee!' said Ah-zed-zo, 'Nowsee!' A wide smile spread over his face as he looked at Anwawd. By chance, Anwawd had said the two words 'Now see', which meant, in the Calusa language, 'splendid one'. Isticáti nodded his approval. Ah-zed-zo went back into the middle of the circle and said, 'Cilo-citá ia,' (which meant, 'The one of strange words is a good man'), and pointed to Anwawd.

They continued with the feast, and had deer meat and vegetables, a large variety of fish, and a clear, sweet drink made with honey. After eating, Ah-zed-zo took out some kind of pipe and filled it ceremoniously with small leaves. He took it to Isticáti, handed it to him and spoke at length. The young man accepted it, said a few words, and then put the stem of the pipe to his lips and, to the consternation of the Welsh, Ah-zed-zo, went to fetch a twig from the fire, brought it to Isticáti, and put it to the bowl of the pipe. The young man sucked until smoke came out of his nostrils.

'He's going to burn his chief,' said Anwawd.

'Perhaps we ought to be ready, in case we too are burnt,' said Tudwal, stealthily looking for a piece of wood or a stone with which to defend himself.

'Our friend here is not burning him,' said Elidir. 'It's some kind of ritual.'

'You're right,' said Madog. 'Don't be vexed,' he said to his men, 'and, above all,' he said to Tudwal, 'don't show any desire to fight.'

After sucking smoke and blowing it out for some time, Isticáti handed the pipe to Madog, who held its long stem and put it to his lips. He sucked and filled his mouth with strong-tasting smoke. He made the serious mistake of swallowing it, and began to cough painfully. His eyes turned red and filled with tears.

'He's burnt his mouth,' said Anwawd, 'and swallowed fire.'

'He's swallowed smoke,' said Elidir to Anwawd. Then he turned to Madog and said, 'Blow out the smoke.'

Isticáti took the pipe from Madog, sucked some more smoke, and made it clear that he blew it out. Then, he returned the pipe to Madog. This time, he sucked the smoke very carefully, and blew it out straight away. He did this several times. Then, Ah-zed-zo took the pipe and handed it to Anwawd, who sucked the smoke carefully and then blew it out in a cloud.

'This isn't half as bad as it looks,' he said, and sucked in again. He was beginning to enjoy himself, when Ah-zed-zo took the pipe from him and gave it to Elidir. And so the pipe went round, from one to the other, in the circle.

Everyone tended to gulp some of the honey drink after smoking. Ah-zed-zo and Anwawd drank copiously and, towards the end of the feast, the two went to stand in the middle of the circle of those eating, and sang and chanted in turn. Anwawd's renditions, where he accompanied himself on the harp, were much applauded, and this pleased him greatly. By the end of the night, he and Ah-zed-zo were such good friends that Anwawd allowed him a turn on his harp; no one remembered this ever happening before.

This was the beginning of life together for the Welsh and the Calusa. The Welsh built cabins for themselves, with the help of the Calusa, and began to learn their language and way of life.

The Calusa were expert fishermen, and they would go out to sea in their canoes, handling them with great proficiency, but they could also catch fish in a very special way. They would dig deep pits on one seashore, so that the sea flowed into them, and then they went out to sea, and, with nets that were long enough to stretch from one canoe to the other over a distance of thirty metres, and by using many canoes in this way, they would drag the nets through the sea and force fish into the pits. Then, they would close the exits from the pits to the sea, and take the fish, whenever they needed them, until the pits were empty – when they would open the pits again and catch more fish in the

same way. The Welsh marvelled at the way the Calusa made use of shells and fish bones, making ear-rings, bracelets and torques out of them.

The Welsh learnt the Calusa way of hunting, as well. This was not difficult, for the, were already familiar with shooting with bows, and setting traps. The most important thing they learned was the way the Calusa tracked animals. They learned to recognize the sounds made by the different birds and animals, to know the grunt of the boar ('*sukf*'), the cry of the eagle ('*lumhe*') whose feathers every chief was anxious to have to wear, and the deadly sound of the rattle-snake ('*cectoracracracat*').

One day, Madog was out hunting with Isticáti. They had wandered far from their camp when they came across six natives from another tribe. Isticáti greeted the six in his own language, which was close enough to their language for them to understand each other. They stared with great interest at Madog, but after being told his story, and hearing the explanation for the colour of his skin and hair, and his blue eyes, they sat down and talked. They were surprised that Madog spoke the Calusa language so well. The six told Isticáti that they had wandered far from their camp, but that they would be welcome to return there with them. It would have been a grave mistake to refuse, for it would have brought disgrace on those who gave the invitation, and so Isticáti and Madog travelled for many days with the six, and came to a land of lush, green growth and blue waters, so that it was difficult to say whether all of it was land, or a great lake with many islands in it. Then the six went to take out their hidden canoes, and it was in these that Madog and Isticáti travelled with them for some hours, until they came to a considerable piece of land, which the men called 'Pa-mai-oki' ('Grassy waters'). Throughout the journey, what impressed Madog was how full of living things the place was. In some places, the air was filled with large butterflies, spectacularly coloured. From time to time, he saw otters, fresh water turtles, and water snakes. The trees were full of the songs of birds. In one place, their six friends began to talk excitedly, saying the word 'Hoolpootoo' and pointing to the water. What they pointed to was a creature like a tree trunk, moving slowly by. They saw it pull itself awkwardly onto the waterside and walk clumsily on four short legs.

At long last, they pulled ashore on a large stretch of land and, after securing the canoes, they came to a camp that was very similar to Isticáti's. They were warmly welcomed. Here again, everyone looked with wonder at Madog. A feast was held. Madog found himself eating several varieties of fish and meats, but he did not understand until later that he had eaten some snake meat. 'Tasted a bit like chicken,' he said to himself.

On his first day in the new camp, Madog was walking about, followed by a gang of children, when he saw a group of women washing clothes in the water. One girl raised her head. Her skin was like dark silk and her black hair reached half way down her back. Madog felt her dark eyes staring at him. She smiled and he smiled. Then the other women said something, and all of them began to laugh. 'These women are very like the women of Gwynedd,' Madog thought, 'always ready to tease each other.' He went on, but turned to look back at the girl. She was still watching him. In Gwynedd, he would have known exactly what he would have done, especially as he was of the line of princes; but here things were different, and he well knew that he could make a mistake that would end in trouble.

When he arrived back at the camp, he had a word with Isticáti. By now, Madog had learnt enough of the Calusa language to cope with most of the important things in his life.

'Today, I saw a girl,' he began.

'You saw a girl yesterday, as well,' said Isticáti, half concealing a smile.

'True; I saw many girls yesterday.'

'Why is today different from yesterday?'

'The girl I saw today was different from all the girls I saw yesterday, and all the other girls I saw today, come to that.'

'Such things happen,' said Isticáti, 'but girls who are different from other girls are likely to cause trouble, besides being an expensive business.'

'I understand that,' said Madog. 'That's how it is with our families in Wales, too. One needs many cows,' here he made a shape to suggest that animal, 'to get a girl.'

'Tatanka?' (that is, 'buffalo') asked Isticáti, who had heard of such animals from some of the men from the great land.

'If that's the word,' said Madog. 'Our word is 'cow'.'

'There's no cow here,' said Isticáti.

'No cow, no girl – is that what you're saying?' asked Madog.

'No. What I'm saying is: without many things, no girl,' said Isticáti. 'Unless, of course, she's not worth anything: that depends on who she is.'

'A girl with skin like silk, and hair, and long black hair, and…'

'That's true of all the girls here,' said Isticáti. 'A name would be of some help.'

'I don't know her name.'

'Ah! Then you won't get far.'

But Madog went further than Isticáti thought, for on the following day, he went out again to the washing place. Alas! She wasn't there. Then a woman of noble proportions went past.

'I thought you couldn't keep away for long,' she said, smiling.

'Keep away?' said Madog, pretending not to know what she meant.

'Is that how it is, really?' said the woman. 'And, more than likely, you have no interest in finding out her name!'

'She? Oh, Her... well.' If Madog were an actor, this would be the poorest performance that anyone had ever seen.

'Her name is Seeta.' (That is, 'fire'.)

'Seeta,' said Madog. 'Seeta.' He heard heavenly music: this was the most beautiful name he had ever heard.

'Her father is Cooloolooste.' (That is, 'Black Fox'.)

This name had hardly any appeal for Madog, but he had to know it.

'Her father is not the world's pleasantest man,' said the woman, 'but precious things can't be won without effort.'

'Seeta, daughter of Cooloolooste; that's her name,' said Madog to Isticáti, later on.

'I don't much care for her father's name,' said Isticáti. 'He doesn't sound very pleasant, to me.'

'Hm,' said Madog.

'But we'll ask the chief whether we can see him.'

'Good,' said Madog.

And they saw the chief.

'He's not the pleasantest man in the world,' said the chief, 'but you're welcome to go and see him.'

When Madog and Isticáti appeared at the door of Cooloolooste's house, they were confronted by a stout man, with sly eyes, whose first question was, 'And what do you want?'

'You have a daughter…' Madog commenced.

'I know that,' said Cooloolooste. 'Sit. In fact, I have three daughters. No boys. No one was ever so unfortunate as I with his children.'

'Oh!,' said Madog, 'then it would not be the end of the world for you if someone were to take Her off your hands?'

'The three are splendid girls. They're worth the world; the whole world.'

'Seeta,' said Isticáti, 'what would you say she's worth?'

'She's worth the most,' said Cooloolooste, and then repeated with heavy emphasis, 'worth the most.'

'If that's so, we're off now then,' said Isticáti, suppressing the protest that was about to fill Madog's mouth. 'Come on,' he said to him, getting up.

'But not beyond the reach of someone… how shall I say… someone who's brave and wealthy,' Cooloolooste hastened to add.

'My friend is brave, and wealthy,' said Isticáti.

'Him!' said Cooloolooste. 'But he's not one of us.'

'Neither am I,' said Isticáti.

'Not of our tribe, that's true enough,' said Cooloolooste, 'but you are one of us. As for him, well…' Isticáti started to get up again.

'Not one of us, it may be, but…' said Cooloolooste.

'Brave **and wealthy**,' said Isticáti.

'Wealthy? There's all sorts of 'wealthy',' said Cooloolooste, 'What sort is he?'

'There are all sorts of girls too,' said Isticáti. 'What sort is this daughter of yours?'

'Of great worth. Very great worth,' said Cooloolooste, glancing at Madog from the corner of his eye.

'What's that?' asked Madog, as Isticáti nudged him in the ribs.

'A good question. A question that needs to be asked,' said Cooloolooste.

'My friend offers six pigs and a sow, a basketful of fat fish, and two stags,' said Isticáti.

Cooloolooste raised his arms, grimaced, and looked to the heavens. 'Six pigs and a sow, a basketful of fat fish, and two stags! Great worth? You, and he, have the gall to offer me *that* for a girl of great worth, very great worth, for Seeta!' And he began to laugh ironically. 'I thought you said he was wealthy! But I'll say this for him, he must be brave – to make such a pitiful offer.'

Isticáti made as if to get up once again, and said, 'Come on, Madog.'

'Ten pigs, three sows, two basketfuls of fat fish, and four stags,' Cooloolooste declared.

Isticáti sat down again, 'Ten pigs! Three sows! What do you think your daughter is, the daughter of the sun?'

'Just as good.'

'Eight pigs, two sows, one basketful of fish, and two stags.'

'Three stags,' said Cooloolooste.

'Alright, then, three stags,' said Isticáti.

'He's had a bargain and a half,' said Cooloolooste, nodding his head in Madog's direction.

'And you've had the son of the chief of a whole country beyond the sea,' said Isticáti.

It took some time to get all the items of the marriage settlement to Cooloolooste, but, at last, the wedding day arrived. The event took place in Seeta's camp, with two medicine men taking part in a colourful and noisy ceremony: Ah-zed-zo and the medicine man of Seeta's tribe. To crown the proceedings, Anwawd sang a praise poem to the happy couple, accompanying himself on the harp. Once again, he received the kind of reception he felt someone of his calibre deserved.

One year later, a son was born to Madog and Seeta. It was then that the sailors realized that Madog was not likely to return to Wales.

'You're going to stay here, then?' Erik asked his friend one day.

'Yes. This is my place now. What about you?' Madog asked.

'Even though this is a good land and these are good people, I'm going back,' said Erik.

'All the men can choose to stay, or come with you,' said Madog.

Enough men to fill one ship chose to return. This was not surprising, for many of the sailors had done as Madog had done, and brought up families in their new country.

All of the sailors, with the help of several of the men of the Calusa, set about preparing one of the ships that had been hidden. The three ships had been overhauled from time to time, during the period that the Welsh had been in the far country. The wood had been carefully greased; the oars, sails and canvases had been repaired and renewed, and additional ones made. The ship that was returning was fitted with a new helm, and provided with plenty of wood in case of any accidents. The ballast was put in place once again. It was loaded with as much food and water as possible, and with many treasures:

various adornments, feather head-dresses of eagle feathers, alligator teeth, the tail of a rattlesnake, bows and knives, and other treasures. Erik and Elidir would be in charge of *Eryn*. Anwawd, too, was on board. He left his harp as a gift for Ah-zed-zo. One May morning, those staying behind said farewell to those sailing. The ship was escorted into the open sea by six canoes, and once it was on the ocean, it was carried by strong currents, and then by strong winds from the west. Whereas the voyage to the far land had taken eight months, the voyage back to Wales took only five.

12

Home to Wales

No-one ever received a welcome like the one the sailors were given when they came back from the far country. Wherever they went, people gathered about them, asking what sort of place was the land across the sea, and what kind of voyage they had. The welcome at the court of Owain Gwynedd was extraordinary, though not everyone was pleased to see them back. People marvelled at the treasures from the far country, and some sailors made a good profit by exchanging their treasures for cows. However, there were three men at court who found it difficult to smile – although they attempted to, in case they annoyed the prince. These three were Cadfan, Crafanc and Beuno. Erik gave an account of their long voyage, mentioning their adventures, and stating categorically that there was no edge to the round world, and that it was not possible to fall off. He described the far country and said that Madog had settled there, and that there would be an opportunity for anyone who wanted to join him to come with him, Erik, on his second voyage, in due course.

But Anwawd was the storyteller *par excellence*; he revelled in describing all things that had happened to the men.

'Those of you here in court who do not remember how things were when we made our heroic voyage,' he said, after a feast one night, 'I'll tell you all about it. Erik here, and

Madog, building ships in a totally new way, thirteen of them, the like of which…'

'Thirteen!' Crafanc complained. 'Thirteen! Can't you count?'

'You needn't be such a crab about minor details,' said Anwawd, 'you need to enter into the spirit of the adventure. As I said, thirteen ships, the like of which no one had ever seen, ships that were like ponies dancing on the waters, in favourable weather, but that were as rugged as rocks, in the great tempests of the sea. Here, you don't know anything about tempests. You call a strong breeze that ruffles the water a storm. What's that compared with what we saw? Mountainous seas, waves like cliffs raising the ship high up in the sky, and then crashing us down to the depths. It was like falling down from heaven!

'And islands! Anglesey, I don't deny, is quite a large island, but what is Anglesey compared with the places we've seen? We saw islands that were as big as countries, full of wonders: men with such big feet that they could take shelter under them when it was raining; creatures that were half snakes and half women, with hair of little snakes; people who carried their heads in their armpits and ate grass. And what about mountains full of great dragons that spat out slabs of burning stones and red-hot rocks about us? If it hadn't been for Madog, and Erik here, expert sailors that they are, we wouldn't be here today, to tell you these things.'

Here Crafanc interrupted him. 'Did you say dragons that spat out fire? Taliesin also saw some of those. Did I tell you of the poem about Taliesin's journey to the land of dragons? It begins like this…'

Anwawd in turn interrupted him. 'Taliesin never saw the things we saw. And, anyway, that was a long time ago, in the darkness of the old ages. I'm talking about now. And neither Taliesin nor anyone else saw the kind of sea we saw; a sea full of seaweed as thick as ropes where, at night, sea-snakes with lights on their bellies swam to the surface, some of them as long as this room, huge, ugly things that encircled our ships and made the water green with their poison. It took a very brave sailor to be there on such a sea, but that was not the worst thing in that horrifying sea. During the night, a dark ship appeared, full of black things like devils with shining eyes…'

This time it was Beuno who interrupted. 'Paul the Apostle also saw such things, things from hell and, by the way, the Apostle suffered many storms at sea, and was always saved by God's angels that came down in a heavenly light to look after him.'

'It may well be that Paul the Apostle saw such things, but these wanted to lure us into a giant whirlpool…'

'I'd call that the edge of the world,' said Cadfan. 'You'd have gone over the edge if you'd…'

'That wasn't the edge of the world at all; it was an enormous whirlpool; there was sea all around it. It would suck you into a watery grave; if you went within reach of the whirling current, you'd be swallowed into the deep, to end up as corpses in a jungle of seaweed, being bitten by giant snakes with lights on their bellies. But we went past the place and reached the most pleasant land that anyone ever saw. There were fruits that bent the trees so that you only had to reach out to find a delicious meal that was enough to last you for a week. The sea was so full of fat fish that all you had to do was to cast a net into the water to catch great slabs of fish that would feed a family for days. And rabbits! The rabbits were as big as hounds, and so easy to catch that a three-year-old boy could do it. And talk about meat! Roasted, it was so tender that it melted in your mouth. All this, lads, besides the heavy deer there, and the masses of birds in the trees. And this is the best thing of all: there was no winter there; it was fine all through the year, apart from the occasional shower to keep down the dust. And such good people! I've never seen better people, living easily and joyfully in this green and pleasant land.'

'Wasn't there anything unpleasant there?' Cadfan asked sourly.

'Oh, yes,' said Anwawd.

'There's a serpent in every Eden,' remarked Beuno, shaking his head and looking wise.

'There were serpents there as well, but you didn't have to worry too much about them; you just left them alone. But there were other things. There's the time when I and Tudwal had gone over to the green swamp where Seeta lived – she became the wife of our Madog. We were in a boat made out of a hollowed tree trunk; the word for this kind of boat is 'canoe'. We saw a tree trunk floating in the water, the back of it all gnarled and rough. Well, a tree is a tree, and that's it. But we saw this trunk moving towards the bank where there were women, and also children playing. Suddenly, the tree trunk opened an enormous mouth full of sharp teeth like a saw, and shut it with a snap on part of a young boy's clothes. He happened to be in the water. Those on the river bank were shocked and alarmed and began to shout like nothing I've ever heard. Tudwal and I rowed like madmen for the shore, and when we were within reach of that living tree, Tudwal leapt into the water, with his knife in his hand, and grabbed this creature. It let the boy go and turned on Tudwal, all terrible teeth! And a fight started. Soon, the water was splashing and churning about the two of them, and this dangerous beast was floundering like nothing you've seen. It was a battle and a half, but at last, Tudwal plunged his knife into the creature's throat where the flesh was tender – the rest of it was as hard as a shield. Once, twice, three times the knife sank into the creature's flesh, and gradually it became still and died. You should see the joy there afterwards. Tudwal and I were heroes and treated like kings.

'The people of the land had their own religion.'

'I see that the church will have to send missionaries there,' said Beuno.

'If I understood rightly, they had some Great Spirit there – Wakan Tanka they called him – instead of our God, and the entire world belonged to him, and the people were supposed to take care of this world, because it belonged to Wakan Tanka.'

'Did they have priests?' Beuno asked.

'Oh yes,' said Anwawd. 'One of the most important in our place was Ah-zed-zo.'

'Ah-zed-zo!' said Beuno. Then he went on mischievously, 'There's a familiar ring to that name!' Everybody else, apart from Crafanc, began to laugh, carefully.

Anwawd added, 'We had people like him – I said so.'

And this is how it was for a long time. Anwawd spun out his stories and was welcomed and fed and given gifts, and enjoyed it all. Erik listened to his tales with as much wonder as everyone else, until he became bored. Then, he set about preparing for a second voyage to the far land; but that's another story.

13

Sun Dance

Five children, three sons and two daughters, were born to Madog and Seeta. After the boys had become young men, Isticáti asked Madog to come with him and Ah-zed-zo on a long, long journey to the north, to attend the Great Meeting of the Tribes. He agreed. Two of Isticáti's sons and two of Madog's sons came with them. As a matter of fact, the Calusa lived on a large peninsula, and what they did was to travel up to a place that Isticáti called 'The Big Country', past a land that the inhabitants called Tallahassee. It was often easier for them to travel by water than over land, and they had light canoes made of skin on a wooden frame for that purpose; they were easy to carry.

By the time they reached the meeting place it was the beginning of summer. Many tepees had been set up on a wide, wide plain, and there were people there, wearing different kinds of clothes, busy by their tepees or walking about. Some wore aprons like Isticáti and his companions, others wore trousers and shirts made of skin, many wore different kinds of feathers in their dark hair, and a few men wore head-dresses full of feathers, feathers that reached half way down their backs. One or two wore bearskins. 'Very hot in this weather,' thought Madog.

Almost everyone turned to look at Madog and his sons because they were so fair, but no one made any remarks. Whilst Madog and Isticáti and their sons were putting together a cabin of wood and leaves, Ah-zed-zo left them and went to the middle of the camp.

When he arrived, he saw six medicine men like himself there. Some of them understood each other's languages, but everyone understood some words of the languages of the others, and they had signs made with the hands that helped them to understand one another. The seven sat in a circle, conversing. A great ritual was about to be performed.

The following day, the seven medicine men met in the middle of the large plain. All the people gathered about them there. The seven sat in a circle and smoked a pipe, each one sucking smoke from it and passing it on to the next. This was the beginning of the ritual. Then they stood up and made the shape of a circle on the ground with a cross in the middle, with the tip of each line pointing to the four directions: north, south, east, and west. In the dead centre, where the lines crossed, they placed eagle feathers, the bird that signified, for them, the whole world's might. Then, one of them began to make a whistling sound with pipes made of eagle bones, whilst others cut the shape of a full moon out of skin, as a sign that light was stronger than darkness, and a picture of 'tatanka' (a 'buffalo') as a sign of all the people of the world.

'Come here, young men,' said Ah-zed-zo. And ten young warriors came to him, including the two sons of Isticáti. Ah-zed-zo gave them sage and told them to follow his directions in marking out the circle for the Dance Pavilion. 'Wear your war-garb,' he added, 'and then go into the forest, to look for a tall and fair poplar tree. After you've found one, come back here.'

After some time, the young men returned, and the seven medicine men followed them back into the forest. After coming to the tree, four of the young men were placed around it, one to the north, one to the west, one to the east, and one to the south, each one with an axe in his hand. To the beat of a drum, the others started to dance around them. As they danced, one of the four young men came near the tree and struck it hard with his axe. The other three each did the same in turn. This was repeated until the tree was ready to drop. Then, the ten young men came to it and cut it free of its stump, taking care that it did not touch the ground while they carried it. As they went towards the camp, they howled like coyotes.

After arriving at the camp and going to the very centre, they stood the tree in a hole that had been dug there. Then their task was to build a large hut around the tree. This would be the Pavilion of the Dance, and would signify the universe. After this, all the warriors of the tribes gathered there, put on their war feathers and painted their bodies. The instruments mainly used in their ceremonies were drums. These began to sound, and the warriors began to dance, shout and scream. By now it was getting dark. The seven medicine men told the ten young men to sit. They sat in a circle, at first, smoking and passing the pipe from one to the other. Whilst this was going on, Ah-zed-zo chanted a prayer, 'O Wakan Tanka,' ('Great Spirit') he said, 'here I'm showing you the circle of our people on your earth. We suffer in order to deserve your light.'

Then the ten young warriors went into the Pavilion of the Dance, and the door was closed. They stayed there till the morning, dancing and sweating profusely, as a sign that they were pure, pure enough to take part in the ceremony. The door was opened briefly and they were given a little water. One of the medicine men went in with them. Then the door was closed for the last time.

Inside the Pavilion, one of the young warriors went into the middle, where the poplar tree was. There the medicine man awaited him, with a knife in his hand.

'You have to suffer for the good of all,' the medicine man said, making two incisions three centimetres apart and four centimetres long. One pair of these incisions were made on the chest, one on the shoulder, and one on the back of this warrior, and the other warriors in turn. Then the medicine man pushed a thin thong beneath the skin made loose by each pair of incisions, so that the warrior was held fast by his skin. Then he tied the two ends of each thong tightly onto the poplar tree. By now, the warrior was tied to the tree by his skin. What happened next was that he had to pull and pull, in great pain, until his skin broke and he was loose. This happened to all the young warriors in the pavilion.

Outside, the drums were beating rhythmically and all the people were dancing in a circle. They carried on all day and far into the night. When the pale light of the sun appeared in the east, the pavilion door was opened in that direction, and the young warriors and the medicine man came out of the pavilion. When this happened, the drumming and the dancing stopped immediately, so that there was an intense and oppressive silence over the whole place. This lasted until the sun grew stronger and it was daylight.

'The light of Wakan Tanka shines on us all,' said Ah-zed-zo. 'He has made the entire world bright. We are joyful now. The world is full of glory.'

Then, several women came forward to wash the young warriors and the medicine man that had been in the Pavilion of the Dance. They put ointment made of herbs on the warriors' wounds.

'The colour of the earth is red,' said Ah-zed-zo, 'and we have all come from the earth.'

Then, the women painted the warriors red from the waist up.

Ah-zed-zo said, 'The colour of despair is black.'

Now all the women painted circles of black about the faces of the warriors, and drew black lines down their noses and their cheeks and chins, and drew black circles around their wounds.

'This is a sign that our wounds set us free from the

darkness of our ignorance,' said Ah-zed-zo.

The drums started to beat again, the sounds of flutes joined in and the dancing recommenced.

'Our ritual is ended. And it is good,' said Ah-zed-zo.

Madog marvelled at all of this. 'There's some kind of god here as well,' he thought. 'I wonder what Beuno would say?' But though he was willing enough to watch their religion, in his heart he still believed in the religion of his own church. Then he began to think that he was a Welshman who was on his way to becoming one of the Calusa, but he and his family, and the Welsh sailors who had stayed with him, still spoke Welsh, as well as the Calusa language.

As had happened to Madog and Seeta, so it happened to their sons. They met women from among the tribes of the north and, in time, they moved up with them. And that is how some people of the Big Country came to speak Welsh. The families of Madog's sons became a tribe that flourished for a long time in the middle of the Big Country, about the river that is called 'Missouri'. They were the Mandan tribe, the tribe of people with blue eyes, who spoke Welsh.

14

The Journey's End

By now Madog was an old man, and Seeta an old woman. Some of their children and grandchildren lived in the same camp as them, but the others had gone far away. Now Madog lived a quiet life, and every day he would sit with the other old men, talking about the old days. His friends liked to hear about Wales, the country from which he sailed, and about his wonderful voyage. One day, Madog was seized by a great urge to see his old ship, *Gwennan Bendragon*, which was slowly rotting where it had been hidden. He told Seeta about this. She did not say much, but she fetched him his sword, the one he had when he came from Wales, just as if she were reading his mind. But she told Isticáti about her husband's intention.

'I'll go with him,' he said. 'It was on that seashore we met for the first time, in the old days.'

The two of them made their way slowly through the wood and the green land, and gradually they came down to the shore.

'The ship's here,' said Isticáti, pointing to some luxuriant growth.

'The place has grown wild,' said Madog. 'I remember a time when we would come down here to tidy up the place, and grease the wood of the old ship.'

'We've grown too old for all that,' said Isticáti, 'and our children have their own things to think about.'

The two of them began to cut the undergrowth, with no particular urgency. As they cut away the green tendrils, more and more of the ship came into view, and more and more memories came back to Madog.

'This is the mast,' he said, holding a long pole by the side of the ship. It broke in three pieces as he tried to lift it.

'Gone soft,' said Isticáti, 'and full of worms eating it up.'

'The oars are in the ship,' Madog remarked, and, after climbing on top of a clump of foliage, he stretched his hand to take hold of one of them. He pulled it out in one piece, and ran his hand along it to get rid of all the rubbish clinging to it. 'Not like new!'

'Nothing's like new, after all these years,' said Isticáti, as he pulled out another oar. 'If we had a boat we could we could put to sea,' he said.

'Rather long, these oars,' said Madog. 'I remember the carpenter, Illtud, whittling away at our first oars, and Erik telling him what to do. Things became rather heated between them. 'Does this young puppy think I'm stupid!' said Illtud throwing his knife into a block of wood so that it quivered, making a whirring sound. But Erik knew his stuff; he knew exactly what kind of oars there were on the ships of the north, and that we had to have oars like them for our journey.'

Madog bent into the boat once more, took hold of an oar and began to pull. The undergrowth had a tight hold on this one and he struggled with it for some minutes before stopping for a breather. Isticáti came over to give him a hand. He grabbed the oar and began to pull. Madog saw a length of something black writhing not far from his friend's

hand. He saw a mouth open, white all about it. For one second he became a young man again. In a flash, his sword was in his hand. He struck. He saw a snake's head fly in the air, clear of its body, before it had a chance to hurl itself forward to bite Isticáti. Then he saw its bloody body turning and writhing in the greenery in the bottom of the ship.

'Moccasin!' said Isticáti, naming the snake. And he knew that his friend had saved his life. Had he been bitten, he was too far from the camp to fetch a medicine man to draw the poison out with his secret herbs.

The two of them left the third oar where it was and went to the seashore, to sit down. Both of them had been severely shaken. Madog's left arm became limp and his sight began to fail.

'What's wrong?' a worried Isticáti asked.

'Not feeling very well,' Madog answered. 'But I'll be better soon, after resting.'

But he wasn't. The world about him seemed to be moving away from him and becoming misty. Isticáti realized what was happening. What was he to do? Should he stay here with his friend, or go back to camp to seek help. What if he went and Madog died here by himself. He decided to stay.

'Let me sit up,' said Madog. There was a smooth stone not far away. Isticáti gently dragged his friend to it, and put him to sit there, with his back resting upon it.

'Am I facing the sea?' asked Madog.

'Yes,' said Isticáti. He well understood that Madog knew that he was embarking on his last voyage. He got up and brought the two oars and set them one on each side of his friend. 'The oars,' he said.

'A sailor's voyage,' said Madog, and smiled painfully.

He began to hear the sound of the sea, as if it were coming nearer. He began to imagine that he saw ships on the waves, full of sailors from Wales. And then he saw Anglesey, and the court of Aberffraw. Then the water turned green, and he felt himself sinking, sinking in a depth that he had never known before.

In due course, some Calusa warriors carried Madog's body to the camp. There, they painted the upper part of his body red and amber. Then they dressed him in his own clothes. The body was placed on a bier, ready to be carried far from the camp. By his side they placed his sword and one of the oars of his ship. And Isticáti added a small wooden cross, because he knew that, for Madog, it was one of the signs of his God. Then the tribe gathered in a colourful procession to carry the bier. Seeta and the son who had stayed in their camp, and their two daughters and all their children walked behind the bier, following Isticáti, their chief. Whilst they were walking from the camp down to a level plain, the drums beat solemnly. After reaching the burial place, they saw that a hole had been prepared there. Madog's body was lowered into it, in the foetal position, and his sword, the oar and the cross were placed there by his side, as well as a skin bag full of water, and some food. Then they threw earth over him, and covered all of it with leafy branches and sweet herbs, to keep away the animals. Then they chanted and prayed to the Great Spirit to watch over him. At length, they all went back to the camp. After this, Madog's name was not uttered for a long time, so that his family would not be pained by memories and longing. Madog was now one of the Ancestors of the tribe, one who could speak to the Great Spirit on behalf of his people.

Today that grave is underneath the parking lot of one of the mammoth supermarkets of southern Florida.

Aftermath

'Madog:' say historians, 'it's a good story, but there's nothing to it,' as they tear it to pieces with facts, one after the other. 'No departure from Wales, no sea voyage, no remains, no grave.' 'One of the tales of the Welsh, a nation that's been sprawled out so long in the dirt, told only to try to make themselves important in the eyes of the world.' 'Ta-ta, Madog.'

However, the research is not complete. A few years ago, a Welsh historian was once again on the trail of Madog, and he had been travelling here and there in America. One day, he came to the Missouri, and there he met a small band of people. These were the remnants of the

Mandan, the descendants of Madog. They were living on a piece of waste land in two caravans that had seen better days, unable to afford houses, and having forgotten how to live in tepees. A couple of pigs rooted around the rubbish that was heaped here and there. All around there were small piles of old tyres, empty Coca-Cola cans, parts of old car engines leaking black, filthy oil into the ground, skeletal televisions, broken fridges, and washing machines. Half a dozen boys and girls were riding around on battered bicycles, in a cold wind, speaking American English and refusing even to acknowledge that they had Mandan names. From one of the caravans, where the television blared out advertisements for American goods that none of them could ever afford, an old man with a furrowed face came out.

'Do you remember anything of the old days?' enquired the historian. As he pulled a woollen shawl tightly about him, he looked at his interrogator.

'Many things, which no one wants to remember now,' he said. Then he added, 'Do you know that there are now less than four hundred of us, the Mandan, in existence. The great circle of our people has been broken; and before long there won't be any of us left, and no one will remember we ever existed.'

'Do you remember a story about a white man from over the sea?' the historian asked.

'There was some talk of that, a long time ago,' said the old man, 'but not now. All talk of him has finished; gone the same way as those things that made us a people: the Sun Dance, the Rite of the Bear, ceremonies that could cure us, and make us strong.'

'Do you remember your old language?'

'I remember. You can't forget your language. But I can count on the fingers of one hand those that can speak it today.'

The two of them, the historian and the old man, walked down to the great river. The old man looked over the waters and, of his own accord and without any persuasion, began to chant an old prayer imploring the Great Spirit to help his tribe. A gleam came to his eye for a second, then he turned and looked at the place where he and his family lived, and the gleam died.

'This is how we are now. We don't ask the Great Spirit for anything any more.'

As he looked about him and as he listened to the old man's words, for half an instant there, the historian imagined he saw an apparition by the riverside. A young man stood there, twenty years of age, tall and strong, with yellow hair and a fair skin, dressed in clothes that were centuries old.

'Madog!' said the historian, and, as he uttered the name, the history of his own people came like a flood into his mind, and he thought that there was something of his own experience in the phantom by the river. 'It may be,' he said to himself, 'that something of my Wales exists, or has existed, in America, after all.' But the phantom faded. It vanished. And then nothing remained except the cold wind that blew from the waste land over the dark waters of the Missouri.